Ratanbai
A High-Caste Child-Wife

Shevantibai M. Nikambe
(Copyright The British Library)

RATANBAI
A HIGH-CASTE CHILD-WIFE

Shevantibai M. Nikambe

with a Preface by
THE LADY HARRIS, C.I.

Edited by
CHANDANI LOKUGÉ

OXFORD
UNIVERSITY PRESS

YMCA Library Building, Jai Singh Road, New Delhi 110 001

Oxford University Press is a department of the University of Oxford.
It furthers the University's objective of excellence in research, scholarship,
and education by publishing worldwide in

Oxford   New York
Auckland   Bangkok   Buenos Aires   Cape Town   Chennai
Dar es Salaam   Delhi   Hong Kong   Istanbul   Karachi   Kolkata
Kuala Lumpur   Madrid   Melbourne   Mexico City   Mumbai   Nairobi
São Paulo   Shanghai   Taipei   Tokyo   Toronto

Oxford is a registered trademark of Oxford University Press
in the UK and in certain other countries

Published in India
By Oxford University Press, New Delhi

© Oxford University Press 2004

The moral rights of the author have been asserted
Database right Oxford University Press (maker)

First published 2004

All rights reserved. No part of this publication may be reproduced, stored in a
retrieval system, or transmitted, in any form or by any means, without the prior
permission in writing of Oxford University Press, or as expressly permitted by law,
or under terms agreed with the appropriate reprographics rights organization.
Enquiries concerning reproduction outside the scope of the above should be sent to
the Rights Department, Oxford University Press, at the address above

You must not circulate this book in any other binding or cover
and you must impose this same condition on any acquirer

ISBN 0 19 566311 X

Typeset in Garamond (TTF) in 11/13
by Excellent Laser Typesetters, Pitampura, Delhi 110 034
Printed in India by Sai Printopack Pvt. Ltd., New Delhi 110 020
Published by Manzar Khan, Oxford University Press
YMCA Library Building, Jai Singh Road, New Delhi 110 001

ACKNOWLEDGEMENTS

My gratitude to everyone involved in this publication: the editors of Oxford University Press for their dedication to the Classic Reissue series and this book; the Faculty of Arts, Monash University for the project completion grant, Ms Sue Forster for research assistance, and Ms Dunya Lindsey for proofreading the manuscript.

Special thanks to Makarand Paranjape, Professor in English, Jawaharlal Nehru University, New Delhi, for the Afterword.

ILLUSTRATIONS

Shevantibai M. Nikambe (Copyright The British Library)	frontispiece
A *Shenvi* Brahmin girl A pupil in Mrs Nikambe's school (Copyright The British Library)	22
A *Konkanastha* Brahmin family (Copyright The British Library)	31
A group of high-caste young Hindu wives In Mrs Nikambe's school (Copyright The British Library)	44

CONTENTS

Note on the Text	viii
Shevantibai Nikambe (b. 1865)	ix
A Chronology of Shevantibai Nikambe	xi
Introduction by Chandani Lokugé	xiii
Ratanbai: A High-Caste Child-Wife	1
Diacritics used in the first edition	60
Afterword by Makarand Paranjape	64
Explanatory Notes	72
'Pandita Ramabai and the Problem of India's Married Women and Widows' by Shevantibai Nikambe	97
Bibliography	106

NOTE ON THE TEXT

Ratanbai: *A High-Caste Child-Wife* was published as *Ratanbai*: *A Sketch of a Bombay High Caste Hindu Young Wife* in 1895 by Marshall Brothers, London. The text printed here is from that edition.

Italicized words and footnotes in the first edition occasionally modified/standardized for accuracy or understanding, have been retained. Typos have been corrected, and & c revised as etc. Diacritics used within the text in the first edition (together with those omitted from it) have been listed at the end of the book.

SHEVANTIBAI NIKAMBE (b. 1865)

There is very little information about Shevantibai Nikambe.[1] A Christian, she was born in Poona and educated at St. Peter's Girls' High School, Bombay, from where she matriculated in 1884. Deeply influenced by Pandita Ramabai's life and career, she joined the staff of Ramabai's Sharada Sadan High School in Bombay in 1890. A Christian institution, the school accommodated high-caste girls, young widows, and, after the great famine of 1896, extended to accommodate destitute children. When the school shifted base to Poona, Nikambe remained in Bombay and gradually established The Married Women's School, meant for high-caste Hindu child-wives, widows, and the wives of professional men. Nikambe mentions that the school was well supported by both the government and the general public, and that, by 1833, in just sixteen years of its existence, it had successfully educated a thousand women.

Nikambe was well acquainted with contemporary educational reforms for women and understood the difficulties that

[1] All the information that follows is from: *Women in India, Who's Who* (Bombay: National Council of Women, 1935), p. 52; Shevantibai Nikambe's one published essay, 'Pandita Ramabai and the Problem of India's Married Women and Widows' in *Women in Modern India*, collected and edited by Evelyn C. Gedge and Mithan Choksi (Bombay: D. V. Taraporewala Sons and Co, 1929), pp. 14–24; and the two prefaces in *Ratanbai*, one by Nikambe, and the other by Lady Ada Harris.

young Indian wives and widows faced in acquiring a formal education. She was also actively involved with relevant reformist organizations, such as the Students' Literary and Scientific Society and was a delegate at the Second All India Women's Conference on Educational Reforms. She also travelled twice to Europe and America to study Christian missionary work and methods as well as educational and social work. Her wide experience and knowledge gained from such an exposure enabled her to develop as a successful educator, benefitting the lives of many Indian women and wives.

A CHRONOLOGY OF SHEVANTIBAI NIKAMBE

1865   Born in Poona.
1884   Matriculates from St. Peter's Girls' High School, Bombay.
1885–90   First headmistress of the Students' Literary and Scientific Society at Aden Girls' School; proprietress and headmistress of the English School for Indian Girls; inspector of girls' primary schools in Bombay.
1889   Attends (with her husband) the opening of Pandita Ramabai's Sharada Sadan High School in Chowpatty, Bombay. Joins the school as a staff member.
1890   Sharada Sadan shifts to Poona, and Nikambe remains in Bombay to establish her own school, The Married Women's School.
1895   Novel *Ratanbai: A Sketch of A Bombay High Caste Hindu Young Wife* is published by Marshall Brothers, London, UK.
1896   Visits Europe and America to study Christian work and methods.
1912–34   Develops The Married Women's School.
1913   Revisits Europe to study educational and social work.
1928   Is a delegate at the Second All India Women's Conference on Educational Reform held in Delhi.
1929   Essay titled 'Pandita Ramabai and the Problem of

India's Married Women and Widows' is published in *Women in Modern India: Fifteen Papers by Indian Women Writers*, collected and edited by Evelyn C. Gedge and Mithan Choksi (Bombay: D. B. Taraporewala Sons and Co), pp. 14-24.

INTRODUCTION

Ratanbai by Shevantibai Nikambe narrates the poignant story of a high-caste eleven-year old Hindu child-wife in later nineteenth-century Bombay. One of the pioneers of the Indian women's literary canon in English, Nikambe is a contemporary of Krupabai Satthianadhan, the author of *Saguna: The First Autobiographical Novel in English by an Indian Woman* (1887–8), and *Kamala: The Story of a Hindu Child-Wife* (1894).[1]

Ratanbai was first published in 1895 by Marshall Brothers, London, who specialized in religious and imperial themes such as stories about missionaries, the British colonies, and oriental locations.[2] The narrative, heavily dotted with a glossary on local words and in-text explanations of local customs, suggests that it addressed a readership unaware of and eager to learn about an exotic culture. Brief reviews published in British newspapers of the first edition of *Ratanbai* exemplify this particular reader interest in tones of pity and/or amusement.[3] The review in

[1] *Saguna* (1887; New Delhi, Oxford University Press, 1998); *Kamala* (1894; New Delhi: Oxford University Press, 1998).

[2] For some of their representative publications, see Explanatory Notes, Note on the Text, *Marshall Brothers, London*.

[3] See for instance, 'Child-Wives in India' in *The Daily News*, London, 20 July 1985, p. 6; 'The Hindu Girl-Wife' in *The Daily Chronicle*, London, Wednesday, 24 July 1895; 'Book World' in *The Christian*, London, 18 July, p. 22. A flier enclosed in a first edition of *Ratanbai* promotes it with brief extracts from the above newspapers and also advertises it as being priced at '75 cents; postage

The Daily Chronicle reads: 'It is amusing and disconcerting to read how, when Ratanbai gained the first prize in her class, while her husband at the same time failed in his BA examination, she was therefore [sic] taken away from school!' In addition, the reviews collectively express strong missionary criticism of Hindu religious and social customs and the longing for their eradication through Hindu conversion to Christianity. The comment in *The Christian* is representative: 'It is a pretty and touching story of a child-wife's trails; raising the deep longing that such lives were illumined by the Gospel.' In her novel, Nikambe describes the domestic routine and distinctive domestic and socio-religious customs of the contemporary Maratha community in vivid detail. A traditional flower ceremony, a pilgrimage to Goa, and a puja for young wives are full of inside information, and often radiate an incandescence as the heroine and her extended family participate in them. In *Indian Fiction in English: An Annotated Bibliography*, Dorothy Spencer commends the sociological focus of the novel, but seems to have missed its gem-like quality: 'This little book,' she writes, 'slight as to plot, is full of incidents which throw light on family life, inter-personal relations, values and attitudes among the Maratha Brahmins.'[4]

More subversively, Nikambe addresses a local readership on the importance of ameliorating the status of the Indian woman, as did her sister writers Krupabai Satthianadhan and Cornelia Sorabji.[5] Through the homely stories of Ratan and the girl-widow Tara, Nikambe confronts three of the most controversial colonialist reforms of nineteenth-century India: child marriage, widowhood, and women's education.[6] These are prominent

---

5 cents extra', and available from the following locations in New York: Mrs Ropes, 11 East 64th Street, New York City; and also Mrs Nikambe, Hephzibah House, 263 West 25th Street, New York City.

[4] Dorothy Spencer, *Indian Fiction in English: An Annotated Bibliography* (Philadelphia: University of Pennsylvania Press, 1960), p. 32.

[5] See Satthianadhan, *Saguna* and *Kamala*, and Cornelia Sorabji, *Love and Life Behind the Purdah* (1901; New Delhi: Oxford University Press, 2003).

[6] See Explanatory Notes, n. 7, *early marriages*; n. 7, *advantages of education*; n. 7, *decent education*; n. 12, *uneducated family*, n. 18, *her duty was to please*; n. 26, *Oh! do not make his wife a widow*.

themes in the novel, and have been sporadically noticed by earlier literary critics. K. S. Ramamurti, for instance, argues that the novel's one redeeming feature is its reformist focus. He writes that *Ratanbai* is 'more a propaganda story than pure fiction, but its appearance was significant since it voiced and espoused the cause of women's education and of the emancipation of the Indian woman'. A claim, agreed upon with some reservation.

Ratanbai is primarily a social novel and comprises the reformist agenda. However, Ramamurti's critique is limited because, unable to access the novel, he was compelled, as were Spencer and many of his predecessors, to base his review on secondary sources.[7] Quite naturally, he follows their trend of cursory review. In fact, the novel's value lies also in the ways in which it is presented. By sketching her fictional characters with suggestive depths, and recording their complex responses to domestic crises, Nikambe develops an intimate and moving story. Simultaneously, through it, she projects a microcosmic view of the elitist Brahmin community in nineteenth-century Bombay,[8] seeking equilibrium in the Indian-British encounter.

In addition, Nikambe sometimes imposes on herself certain restraints that prevent her, the author, from affording her characters their much-desired epiphanies in crises, and then the novel turns murky with evocative silences. The silences surround, on the one hand, the conservative Hindu girl's surrender to tradition when her cherished desire is to blossom in new ways in the atmosphere of colonialist reform, and her parents' (and guardians') incapacity to help her. On the other, they are about the subterranean challenges faced by the writer herself as she negotiates the Indian-British encounter for her protagonist. These underwritten, less obvious attributes enrich the text, and provide scope for individual reader interpretation.

[7] For more information on the problems of accessibility, see, Chandani Lokugé, 'The Genesis of the Indian Women's English Literary Tradition: Fostering Interest and Research' in Cynthia vanden Driesen and Satendra Nandan (eds), *Austral-Asian Encounters from Literature and Women's Studies to Politics and Tourism* (New Delhi: Prestige, 2003), pp. 296–304.

[8] See also Explanatory Notes n. 9, *Bombay* and Afterword by Makarand Paranjape.

But first, let us draw out the strengths of *Ratanbai* as a social novel. At this stage, an introduction to Nikambe's own reformist convictions is appropriate as they are faithfully inscribed into the novel. Nikambe's preface to *Ratanbai* suggests that she was a committed anglophile. She humbly and effusively acknowledges her debt of gratitude to Queen Victoria for permitting her to dedicate the novel to 'Her Majesty'. In the same vein, she elaborates on India's indebtedness to England 'whose happy rule in [her] native land is brightening and enlightening the lives and homes of many Hindu women'. Further, her conversance with the English language and the novel form confirm that she belonged to the segment of Indian society most exposed to and influenced by westernization.

In what seems to be her one published essay (1929) titled, 'Pandita Ramabai and the Problem of India's Married Women and Widows' (1929), Nikambe provides us with a summary of her own educational ideologies and the strategies that she used to promote them. The essay details that, deeply influenced by contemporary western women's education and Pandita Ramabai's reformist work, Nikambe developed a career as an educator of high-caste Hindu wives and widows. In the running of her own school, which exclusively accommodated high-caste wives and widows, she followed a popular reformist strategy that was employed by contemporary 'reformed' Indians. Although it contained many western features, this reform movement was generally anxious to remain loyal to its cultural and religious past. It renounced the evils of latter-day Hinduism such as idolatry, polygamy, and sati; idealized the ancient Vedic past; and appealed to the Vedic traditions to support its reforms. Two organizations were particularly active in establishing indigenous religious sanction for women's reform: the Brahmo Samaj (launched in 1828 by Bengali Hindus), which was especially concerned with the reform of the 'enslaved Indian woman' through prohibitions on widow remarriage and female education; and the Arya Samaj (first established in Bombay, in 1875) which was based on recalling Hinduism to its pristine purity. By these means, the women's movement became 'naturalized' as it were, within the Indian society. Among various reforms, the remarriage of widows was legalized in 1856. In 1860, the age of marriage for girls was raised to ten years; in 1891, to twelve years. When effectively exercised, each of these reforms helped in the spread of women's education that, in consequence, facilitated their liberation. However, as is to be expected in a tradition-ridden society, the educational and social reforms took a long time to gain strength. The more traditional Hindus, entrenched in orthodoxy, rejected the notion of the 'New Woman'[9] who would be created by the reforms related to child marriage, sati, widowhood, and women's education. As late as 1882-3, the Education Commission provided proof of the anti-liberation movement waged by the orthodox elites.[10]

As mentioned above, Nikambe subscribed to the theory of the 'reformed party'. In her essay (mentioned above) she glorifies the Indian wife as the 'priestess' of the 'sacred temple of her home'. To support her argument she draws from the great Indian heroines down the ages like Sita, Draupadi, Savitri, and Mirabai whose intellectual and moral strengths were harnessed not for their own self-development but for selfless and sacred service within the shrines of their homes. She upholds her strongest career influence, the learned Pandita Ramabai, shrouded in widowhood and dedicated to educating Indian wives and widows, in line with these heroines, and as a glowing example to the contemporary Indian woman. Only education, Nikambe

---

[9] New Woman: The term applies, in this Introduction, to the Indian woman who emerged in the latter part of the nineteenth century as a consequence of British colonialist influences that included educational and socio-religious reforms. Defying institutionalized patriarchal ideologies that enforced her domesticity and subjectivity, the New Woman sought greater equality between men and women. The value of women as educated and self-reliant individuals, and active participants in domestic and public life comprised the most importants ingredients of the later nineteenth-century ideal. See also, Forbes, 'The "New Woman" of the Late Nineteenth Century', *Women in Modern India*, pp. 28-30, 64-5. See also, n. 7, *decent education*.

[10] Education Commission of 1882-3 as cited in Muriel Wasi, 'Education' in Tara Ali Baig (ed.), *Women of India* (Delhi: Ministry of Information and Broadcasting, Govt. of India), p. 157.

insists, could draw out the full potential of the Indian wife and mother, or widow, and provide her with the resources essential for serving her home and country. Nikambe does not oppose the traditional feminine image of selfless service, but argues to liberate the Indian woman from those institutions that suppressed that service. An educated widow, for instance, if trained in a vocation like teaching or nursing, could 'consecrate her life to some special service for her country, such as has been rendered in the West by sisterhoods or cloisters'.[11] Nikambe is, thus, a diplomatic rather than radical educationist. Her reformist educational programme was based on working through, rather than against, traditional ideology.[12] In her Preface to *Ratanbai*, Lady Ada Harris notes this strategy that Nikambe employed in her school. She commends Nikambe's attempt to educate the high-caste Hindu girls who were usually prevented, by caste taboos and early marriages, from attending school after twelve years of age, but hints that the 'not too engrossing' school curriculum seemed to aim at aiding the students to reach an elevated status as 'happier and better' homemakers and mothers rather than as self-developed individuals.

Nikambe creates several representatives of contemporary Hindu society to debate the hotly controversial reformist issue of her day: women's education. Among the more significant are Mr Vasudevrav, the liberal; Anandibai, his wife; Kakubai, the representative of orthodoxy; Ratan, the child-wife whose maturing consciousness is continually being influenced by these two forces; and the tragic young widow, Tarabai. Skilfully sketched, they are effective stereotypes but memorable as individuals.

Vasudevrav is a paradigmatic example of the split-personality resulting from the Indian-British encounter. He combines the

[11] See the full text of 'Pandita Ramabai and the Problem of India's Married Women and Widows', pp. 97–105. As far as I am aware, this is Nikambe's one published essay.

[12] Nikambe was not alone in using this strategy to promote women's education through contemporary English fiction. See for instance, the prose and fictional publications of Satthianadhan (*Miscellaneous Writings*, *Saguna*, and *Kamala*), and Sorabji (*India Calling*, and *Love and Life Behind the Purdah*).

oriental and occidental in dress and lifestyle. He is one of the 'reformed party'.[13] A lawyer with the High Court, he is in control of his public life in ways that are authorized by the polemics of westernization. That, together with his constant professional contact with the British, possibly account for his partiality towards some features of western lifestyle that he exhibits in public. There is, however, no mention in the novel of his entertaining a single British friend or colleague in his house.[14] What is mentioned is his returning home late one evening after attending a lecture in the 'Hindu Club', suggestive of a social life that did not include his wife. The metaphor of the creaking English boots juxtaposed against the 'Hindu Club' reiterates Vasudevrav's straddling of two cultures. The 'Hindu Club' itself is suggestive of a cultural hybrid, the ways in which the Indians appropriated the British custom of socializing. His mode of travel, described quite à la Jane Austen, replicates the classical and aristocratic social style:

The carriage—a handsome landau, drawn by a pair of fine white horses, a gift from one of the clients—came to the door... With two footmen at the back of the carriage, and a messenger by the coachman's side, they drove through the crowded, busy streets. After ten minutes the carriage stopped. One of the footmen not in livery jumped down...

Vasudevrav ushers the western lifestyle into the outer precincts of his home. His office (in his house) exhibits all the trappings of western comfort. Yet, the room is untastefully and inelegantly furnished: 'portraits of great men mostly literary, hang in a most uncomfortable fashion high up against the roof'. This is because

---

[13] See n. 38, *'reformed'* party.

[14] This illustrates contemporary realities in social interactions between Indians and the British. Many Anglo-Indians complained that they rarely visited Indian households and that the main barrier was the Indian woman. To cite just one telling comment: '...it was this question of [Indian] women. You could have an Indian official... who would come to your house, but you would never go to his, if he was married. You would never meet his wife... You were friends with the chap in office, but you would never be friendly family wise.' For a discussion of this point of view, see Mary A. Procida, *Married to Empire: Gender, Politics and Imperialism in India, 1883-1947* (Manchester: Manchester University Press, 2002), pp. 176-8.

the clerk, who is responsible for the arrangement of the office room, 'though a clever and an honest man, [knew] nothing about making a room attractive'. It is interesting to note that this particular room was furnished by his clerk, and not by his wife. This seems to suggest that Vasudevrav's wife was not actively involved with his professional life.

Nothing in Vasudevrav's dress or demeanor betrays the slightest western influence when he enters the interior of his home, particularly the dining room. Nikambe's description of Vasudevrav at breakfast is an eloquent disclosure of his whole-hearted submission to the reign of local tradition in his domestic environment. The dining room is traditionally furnished, formal, clinically clean, and 'dismal looking'. Vasudevrav himself wears the traditional thread of Brahmanism, traditional clothes and adornments. His wife is essentially the product of Hindu tradition as she 'gently and modestly steps in', sits on the floor and serves her husband who is seated on the stool. The food that is served is as conservative as is the communication (or lack of it) between the husband and wife during the meal.[15]

The tangible accounts of his apartments—office and home—reveal Vasudevrav's adoption of western values to the point of indulging in a luxurious lifestyle; simultaneously, he is shown to submit to an orthodoxy too strong to be resisted. Home and office, then, are the measure of competing cultural influences in his psyche. His mode of attire when he daily takes leave of his domestic life to assume his public role bears witness to this bi-cultural phenomenon that was popularly developed by the contemporary westernized educated Indian elite. He dons a 'long white coat and trousers, with a handsome red turban', but wears 'English boots'. Thus, even while adopting the values of 'superiority, progress, decency, refinement, masculinity and civilization',[16] represented by British dress, he makes the effort to retain his Indian identity. This could well have earned him

---

[15] In traditional Hindu homes, the wife's duty is to serve her husband before partaking of her own meal.

[16] Emma Tarlo, *Clothing Matters: Dress and Identity in India* (Chicago: University of Chicago Press, 1996), p. 48.

some contempt from both the more conservative Hindus and the British. The consequence of all this is that Vasudevrav, like many western-educated and most 'progressive' males of the time, is compelled to live a double life. In his public life, he could be labelled a *baboo*[17] but he returns home to women who cling determinedly to tradition.[18]

Vasudevrav's commitment to some western ideas, especially to education as a means of liberating both men and women from orthodox restrictions, is repeatedly emphasized in *Ratanbai* and represents the authorial view. And yet, Vasudevrav fails to implement his convictions in any effective way, and at this point, the authorial point of view shifts to subtle critique. As the head of his household, Vasudevrav takes the matter of his daughter's education into his hands and, disregarding orthodox prejudices, sends her to school. However, he makes no protest when Ratan is kept away from school by her mother to participate in traditional social and religious activities, and proves ineffectual when her mother succumbs to pressure from Ratan's in-laws who oppose female education, and removes Ratan from school.

[17] The epithet *babo* or *baboo* was applied only to the 'collateral relatives' of royal families of India before British rule. During earlier British rule, English-educated Brahmins engaged in secular pursuits were addressed as baboo. During the latter period, the epithet was applied in derogatory ways to Hindus who attempted to appropriate western dress. The stigma attached to 'babooism' is not an issue addressed in the novel, and this seems appropriate considering Nikambe's novelistic purpose and her readership.

[18] The following is the documented protest of a contemporary, Pratap Chandra Mazumdar:

We go one way, our old relatives another, and our women yet another; and notwithstanding all these conflicting forces, the Indian home remains pretty much in the same condition as it occupied before the government opened its schools and colleges. Our educated young men discuss their projects of reform in debating clubs; but as soon as they get home, they carefully put their progressive ideas in their pockets and bend their necks beneath the yoke of custom as their ancestors before them. They belong to the nineteenth century, but their homes to the first century.

Cited in L. S. S. O' Malley (ed.), 'General Survey', in *Modern India and the West: A Study of the Interactions of their Civilizations* (1941; rpt. London: Oxford University Press, 1968) p. 789.

He submits lamely to the authority vested in orthodoxy instead of repudiating 'the arrangement' that 'had to be fulfilled'. Later, he openly declares his views on education for women but is unable to impose his ideas in his own home when opposed by the ideology of tradition:

...for I am in favour of our girls and women being educated. If some lady were to open a class for the married ladies, I would be the first to send Anandi [his wife]. I am thinking, however, of getting a native lady to come to my house and teach her. If Ratan were in my charge, I would send her to school to-day. I would not have allowed her to be kept at home at this early age, when she was getting on nicely, too; but our girls are not ours when married!

Nikambe's portraits of the two women in the novel, Anandibai and Kakubai, are faithful reproductions of a potent nineteenth-century Hindu woman's persona—of the woman herself as the most persistent barrier to women's reforms. Anandi and Kaku are opposed to their own liberation as much as to that of the next generation.[19] Anandi, Ratan's mother, is a staunch devotee of Hindu orthodoxy. Where she is mistress, as in her kitchen and dining room, tradition is the ruling force: in dress, in meals, in participation at religious festivals, she strictly adheres to it. However, she is seen to react somewhat confusedly between two strong conflicting forces. On one hand, her husband attempts to promote western ideology; on the other, his cousin, the widowed Kaku who lives with them, consistently insists on orthodoxy. Anandi is swayed by their stronger personalities and by a deep concern for her daughter's happiness. What ensues is the insecurity, confusion, and conflicting emotions of cross-cultural conflict. Finally, at the fanatical opposition of Kaku (and of Ratan's in-laws) to women's education, Anandi persuades her husband to terminate Ratan's education. Anandi's

---

[19] See for instance, the trials and tribulations that Russundari Devi or Ramabai Ranade suffered at the hands of the elder women in their households for aspiring to educate themselves. Russundari Devi, *Amar Jiban* (*My Story*), pp. 199–202; Ramabai Ranade, 'Memories of Our Life Together,' trans. Maya Pundit, in Susie Tharu and K. Lalita (eds), *Women Writing in India: 600 BC to the Present*, Vol. 1, *600 BC to the Early 20th Century* (New York: The Feminist Press, 1991), pp. 283–4.

speech and actions in connection with her daughter's education open up complex interpretations. By her own admission, she is caught within the double bind of tradition which encourages opposition to change and demands obedience to one's husband: 'I admit there is no good to be got [in educating a girl] but it is Ratan's father's doing.' And she lets Ratan continue schooling. But it is also because of her decision that Ratan is removed from school. While she publicly announces that she cannot go against her husband's wishes or decisions, this incident projects the Hindu wife as the custodian of orthodoxy who, in its defence, could exercise subversive power within the family.

The dominant force in the household, then, is tradition, and Kaku is the dehumanizing medium through which the writer directly exposes the inflexible attributes of orthodoxy. She is portrayed as the vehicle of such orthodox obsessions as venerable custom, sacrosanct taboo, and fear of defilement. Immersed in traditional Hindu religious and social mores, she is the most active rebel of women's liberation in the novel. Her manifestations of tradition exclude all things new. The author concludes: 'Kakubai is shocked at new ways in the family. She does not like the idea of Ratan's going to school, nor does she approve of [the girl widow] Tara's education, nor of Ratan's husband's going to England.' When she realizes that Ratan is being educated in a formal western-oriented school, Kaku's protest is representative of the orthodox Hindu response to contemporary Indian women's reforms, triggered as much by obsessions with gender demarcations as by racist superiority.

What are you going to do by learning? Are girls going to business now, and will you ask your husbands to mind the home?
 I cannot think what enjoyment the girls find in going to parties. Why do we want all this? It is not so very essential. Did we have these enjoyments in our days? And yet we grew up and prospered. Where did we go to school? Did we even handle a book? We went to the temples daily and worshipped Maravti. We did household work, and attended to *veni phani* [the toilet]. The girls of these days want to go to school, to parties, to sabhas, and eat fruit from the *mlench* [unclean] hands. It is true the Brahmin served, but it was in the house of English people. We are Arya, but our Aryanism is getting all defiled. People are mad after English. Who are these English? Are they not incarnations

of monkeys? Only the tail is not allowed them. What if they are rulers? We must not forget our caste and religion! Truly sin is raging, and the world is coming to an end. Oh Narayan! do thou open the eyes of the people!'[20]

The child Ratan is brought up in this discordant atmosphere that results from the continuous clash of cultures. The dual structure of values, constantly at variance within her home, shapes her consciousness. It is the local lullaby that lulls her to sleep. Religion and religious festivals are given top priority at home and her mother insists on Ratan's full participation in them. Thus, she is given sound instruction in the basics of Hindu tradition. Simultaneously, her father, and more significantly, her school, introduces Ratan to western values and ideas. The frequent references to English poetry (Ratan's favourite subject), and to spoken and written English lessons, suggest that the education imparted by Ratan's school is western-oriented. However unconscious as she is of the indigenous and western value codes, they form an integral part of Ratan's psychological make-up as exemplified in the following leisure activity:

Ratanbai took out a piece of needlework, and in the office room awaited the return of her father. She merrily hummed one of the infant school tunes, and was then singing softly a Sanskrit *shloka*...

Nikambe gives considerable space to the description of Ratan's education. The fictional school, obviously modelled on the institution of which Nikambe was headmistress, puts into practice her educational reforms. The mode of education is western-oriented, but the school is careful to accommodate the traditional Hindu codes of ideology in dress and custom. Photographs are interspersed between the pages of *Ratanbai*, and they all advertise students, a family (possibly a student's), and Nikambe herself (who was headmistress of the school) in traditional dress. Nikambe's descriptions of the school evoke a congenial atmosphere, while brief allusions to elements in the

[20] Fears about gender role reversals were common in contemporary Britain too. The British popular press regularly lampooned female emancipationists as pseudo-men. *Punch* caricatured the New Woman as an untidy and ugly woman who tried to dominate men. The idealized New Woman was single, well educated, and strong-minded, and sought a white-collar or professional job.

curriculum would seem to extol their edifying content. In its own way, the school represents its own inflexible conventions to which individual liberty is subordinated in order to convert it into a 'higher exchange rate' of social freedom. The redeeming factors are that Ratan thoroughly enjoys school, and that it stimulates her intellect. Special mention is made of the poem 'Casabianca' by Felicia Hemans that celebrates a little boy's faith in and unquestioning obedience to his father, and of 'Meddlesome Metty' by Ann Taylor that warns little girls against being inquisitive and inquiring. Thus, Nikambe demonstrates to her local readership that the school selected its teaching material wisely and that it was committed to inculcating good moral values in the students. The novel could also be seen as her effort to educate her students and their families discreetly in the English language and British culture. An interesting detail that corroborates this contention is Ratan's letter to her school friends. It is a model letter, reproduced with the obvious intentions of instructing readers in the finer British art of letter-writing, and in the significance of education. This use of popular fiction to impart practical education to ignorant readers links Nikambe with both contemporary Indian writers of local literature and with the foreign Christian missionary writers of English fiction.[21]

Ratan postulates a model of conduct for others to emulate. She is shown to be the ideal student—clever, eager for knowledge, well-behaved, and beloved of her teachers—and a cut above all the other students. At the same time, Nikambe makes a point of calling attention to Ratan's docility and her femininity, stressing that such vital aspects of the orthodox Hindu personality were nurtured in the students by the school.

However, the author's fictional 'program' for her heroine's psychical development through education is in conflict with the expectations and dictates of that orthodox society of which Ratan is an integral part. The culturally sanctioned code of feminine behaviour stands between Ratan and her desire for

[21] See Meenakshi Mukherjee, *Realism and Reality: The Novel and Society in India* (New Delhi: Oxford University Press, 1985), pp. 34–5.

education both in her own home, and in the sasar's (the father-in-law's house), where Ratan is required to spend a considerable amount of time. Nikambe demonstrates how it restricts and immures the female inner-self. It requires Ratan to surrender to the traditional role of wife as *pativrata*,[22] and insists that she be trained in routine household duties, a process that is seen by the writer as intellectually frustrating and restricting. Nikambe emphasizes its triviality: 'sitting idly for hours, helping to clean the vegetables and grain, gossiping with the neighbouring girls of her age, listening to all sorts of talk of the elderly women were Ratan's usual occupations at the *sasar*'. Nikambe, thus, impacts on the reader that anyone with the faintest of New Woman aspirations would suffer alienation in the conservative Hindu community that offered no inducements for them.

Four months passed, and Ratan's life grew dull and cheerless. She did not know how to while away the time without books or some sort of pleasant occupation. She did attend to the household duties: sometimes she sat cleaning the rice, sometimes sewing, or she had to make the sweets; but literally, her day was mostly spent in doing nothing. At the mother-in-law's, she would simply sit through the long hours of the day with her mother-in-law and the other ignorant lady, and they would stare out of the windows from time to time or fall asleep on the mat. Ratanbai was most miserable and she longed to be at school. How often, with an aching heart, she would sit dreaming about the school life! Her teacher, her companions, her singing lessons, the English lesson, the translation class, came before her and then the longing would come. 'Oh could I but go to school once again.'[23]

Ratanbai develops into a site of protest as Nikambe highlights and critically evaluates the adversities of femininity, and the frustrations imposed on a female inner-self by role identity. Interestingly, this aspect of the novel reflects the paradigm of the women's version of the early western Bildungsroman which develops the tragic figure of the clever and aspiring young

---

[22] See n. 12, *uneducated family*.

[23] For a similar unveiling of the domesticities (in this case for women in purdah) that forced intelligent and aspiring young Indian wives into inertia, see for instance, Satthianadhan, *Kamala*, and Sorabji, 'Love and Life' and 'Behind the Purdah' in *Love and Life behind the Purdah* (New Delhi: Oxford University Press, 2002), pp. 40–9, and 70–80.

heroine who 'sets forth with wit and intelligence only to be punished by an internalized form of self-torture with which she programmes herself into atrophy and disuse'.[24]

The excessive force on gender as a determinant of role, power, and opportunity is another major contemporary women's issue that is taken up in the novel. The intellectual development of the male, Prataprao, is not discouraged even by orthodox society. In spite of being conditioned by male role-identities, he has that inherited power of the male in a patriarchal society to help him achieve his desires, in this case, to be educated. Affirming her belief that education leads both to self-definition and self-development, Nikambe paints a glowing portrait of the educated Prataprao. His personality is transformed by the type of education he receives at Wilson College.[25] The school is western oriented and enables him to perceive the best of the two different cultures and to absorb them harmoniously (as Ratan is shown to do). The writer is careful to stress that Prataprao's appropriation of western attire and ideologies had no adverse effects on the performance of his orthodox duties or on his roles as son and brother:

Prataprao attended Wilson College, and here the sound education he received and the exemplary lives he came in contact with day after day, made a great impression on his young heart, and prepared him for the life before him.... He dressed, like all Hindu students, in a *dhotar* [the Hindu gentleman's dress] and long coat. His head was always covered with the prettiest of embroidered caps. He wore his *bikbali*, and gold ring, and his dear father's gold watch and chain. He was very fond of his mother, and respected her much. His first two sisters and a younger brother loved their *dada* [elder brother] and looked up to him as a pillar in the family now, since their father's death.

The relationship that develops between Prataprao and Ratan is a hard-hitting illustration of the injustices to which a wife could be subjected, in an orthodox Hindu marriage. As discussed above, the traditional role-identity of a wife that is imposed on Ratan excludes any feminist possibilities of self-development. She has

---

[24] Annis Pratt with Barbara White, Andrea Lowenstein and Mary Wyer, *Archetypal Patterns in Women's Fictions* (Sussex: John Spiers, 1982), p. 31.

[25] See n. 13, *college*.

no choice but to suppress her own desires and aspirations. Added to that, she is now expected to merge her identity with her husband's and to direct her mental and moral capabilities towards promoting his happiness. The insinuation is that Prataprao's position is threatened by his wife's higher intellectual potential, and therefore it must be curbed. Despite his failure at examinations, Prataprao is encouraged to continue with his education while 'selfish' Ratan is forced to remain at home, 'pray to the gods, go to temples and pay the vows' to ensure him success. When, by some ingenious manipulation of events, Nikambe makes it possible for Ratan to continue her education, orthodoxy resorts to popular superstitions,[26] and even to dishonesty in order to protect tradition and to persecute her. The old ignorant voice of tradition (in this case the widow Vitha) exclaims:

> School! School! School! Wait, let Prataprao come this evening, I will tell him that I saw you looking at the gardener with an evil eye, and then after your mother-in-law comes to know of it we shall see how you will go to school.

Nikambe asserts that, but for the 'reformed' male voice in the novel playing *deus ex machina*, Ratan's fate would have been as non-productive as that of the ignorant women in the sasar's house, dozing away their void existence upon a mat on the floor. Ratan's education is continued to its desired end only because of the intervention of her husband who insists on it. The potential of the male voice as an advocate for female liberation in this patriarchal society, and the urgent need for change in the traditional female outlook, are recommended by the writer. Unfortunately, after re-establishing Ratanbai firmly on the path to liberation through the provision of education, the writer rushes the novel to a close, leaving out five years of the heroine's life. All loose ends are neatly tied up with the formal marriage ceremony of Ratan and Pratrapao, with which the novel ends.

The personal afflictions of Hindu widowhood[27] and the gender norms that spell disaster for the widow constitute the other

---

[26] Reference to the popular belief that learned women were immoral. See also n. 18, *her duty was to please...*

[27] See n. 26, *Oh! do not make his wife a widow.*

Introduction

contemporary controversial issue on women's reforms that is confronted in the novel. The lovely young widow, Tara, is shown to be the passive recipient of abuse as a result of social norms that determine the attitude adopted towards her by her in-laws and their servants:

> Out of the second carriage a most astonishing and pitiful figure stepped out, and seated herself on the ground, weeping loudly. Then, bending her head, which was shaved but covered with her *padar* [the end part of the sari], she knocked it against a huge stone, and became desperate with grief.... The young widow again knocked her forehead against a stone in desperate grief. She would have indeed preferred to have followed her husband on the funeral pile. Her life was a blank now. The light—the god of her life—was no more. 'What is the use of living!' thought she. She fell backwards and appealed to the god of death. 'Oh Death! Carry me away,' exclaimed the poor, stricken creature; and with the last word she fainted away. For two hours there was utter confusion, and no one would ask her to come in—not even the servant; and there she sat on the bare ground, crushed with grief, until she fainted away... a sight of pity and misery.

Orthodoxy's derogatory attitude towards the Hindu widow is revealed through the response of Tara's immediate relatives to her plight. As expected, the most scathing remarks that reduce her to a social zero, and an harbinger of ill luck, are made by the widow Kaku: 'The wretch has swallowed our Dinu! Why did she marry him? To eat him up in this way! Why hast thou brought this ill luck into the house! She will surely swallow someone here. Our Dinu has gone, and she is nothing to us now.' The author's liberal standpoint regarding this issue is disclosed through Vasudevrav and his daughter Ratan, two of the few people in the novel portrayed as being sensitive to human suffering. Significantly, they represent the ideology of the 'reformed party'. Later, Vasudevrav himself is widowed. However, being male, he escapes the stigma that is considered by society to be Tara's due. Ironically, Tara is blamed for his wife's death, just as she was considered to be the cause of her own husband's death. By her very presence in this house, Tara has brought ill luck; she is the cause of its misery. Deliberately highlighting the inequities of traditional gender norms, the author elaborates on how Vasudevrav is not held responsible for his wife's death and remains master of his house, receiving condolences from friends and relatives.

Thus, it can be concluded that *Ratanbai*, like the contemporary novel, *Kamala* by Krupabai Satthianadhan, is a novel of social protest, committed to exposing the adverse effects of restrictive orthodoxy on contemporary womanhood. Both novels follow the trend of the Bildungsroman by women writers, and Annis Pratt's authoritative remarks about the genre provide for them a relevant declaration of issues:

> In the woman's novel of development... however, the hero[ine] does not *choose* a life to one side of society after conscious deliberation on the subject; rather, she is radically alienated by gender-role norms *from the very outset*. Thus although the authors attempt to accommodate their heroine's *Bildung*, or development, to the general pattern of the genre, the disjunctions... inevitably make a woman's initiation less a self-determined progression towards maturity than a regression from full participation in adult life. It seems more appropriate to use the term *Entwicklungsroman*, the novel of mere growth, mere physical passage from one age to the other without psychological development.[28]

And yet, contrary to the generalization arrived at by Pratt, that all novels of development must inevitably end with the 'growing down' of the heroine, *Ratanbai* sheds a ray of hope on the future of the female. Soon after their formal marriage ceremony, Ratan and her husband are seen to communicate with each other as equals. The novel concludes with the wife being promised more intellectual and spiritual freedom than a traditional patriarchal marriage permits. Nikambe does not hesitate to emphasize that this equity has been (and can only be) reached in marriage if both husband and wife have attained the liberty of mind and spirit to which education paves the way. At the close of the novel, Nikambe makes special mention of a 'beautifully bound gilt-edged Book' that is to guide young people through life. This could be an indirect promotion of Christianity as Nikambe herself was a Hindu converted to Christianity. As the author biography has already revealed, we know that Nikambe was greatly influenced by Pandita Ramabai, and that she was also a member of Ramabai's staff in the school in Bombay. However,

---

[28] Pratt, *Archetypal Patterns*, p. 36.

Christianity is not one of the issues raised in the novel, nor is it mentioned as a subject in the curriculum. This is possibly due to the fact that Nikambe's educational inspiration, Pandita Ramabai, was heavily criticized by the Bombay community for attempting Christian reform in her own school in Bombay,[29] a fact that Nikambe studiously avoids mentioning in her essay on Ramabai. Instead, Nikambe concentrates on the promotion of education throughout the novel, and is also careful to show the highest respect for Brahminism and its distinctive features. It is thus plausible to speculate that 'the Book' symbolizes education.[30]

Meanwhile, Nikambe manoeuvres the external events of the story in such a manner that the young Tara is granted a brighter future than a widow in a strictly orthodox family can ever hope for. Saved from suicide by a Hindu reformer, she is sent away (of course with the sanction of Vasudevrav) to a home for widows to be trained as a teacher. Nikambe's aspirations for the Hindu widow are transparently revealed in her celebration of Tara's new personality that carefully retains the traditional asceticism of Hindu widowhood even while shedding the stigma traditionally attached to it:

Tarabai is still in the Home, where she has studied and been trained as a teacher. She looks very sweet in her 'reformed' dress. Her hair has grown again. Her head is no longer covered, but like the other ladies she wears her padar on the shoulder. She has no *kunku* and no ornaments, not even glass bangles. She wears a print jacket, and puts on a shawl when out of doors.

There is ample evidence that in the above extract, Nikambe is voicing popular strategies used by contemporary reformers to

[29] See n. 56, *Widows' Home*.
[30] The ideal that education is the initial basis of happiness in marriage has been espoused by many contemporary 'novels of purpose' written in Indian languages. Meenakshi Mukherjee analyses the novels of two writers of Indian fiction, Gauri Dutt and Nazir Ahmad, who considered education as a prerequisite for familial bliss. Mukherjee shows that while each of their literate heroines radiates 'cheer and prosperity' within their families, their 'foolish and ignorant' women characters affect family life adversely. The lesson that Gauri Dutt dispenses through his 'instructive' fiction is that 'when the man is literate and the woman is not, there can be no meeting of the minds'.

promote education for Brahmin widows. It is possible that the widows' school, attended by the fictitious Tara was, in reality, the widows' home established by Pandita Ramabai in Bombay and later transferred to Poona. In fact, Nikambe's ideological principles regarding the education of Hindu widows, quoted below, replicate these principles famously advocated by Ramabai.

Every girl's natural ambition is to possess her own home, but if she should become a widow her life can be consecrated to some special service for her country, such as has been rendered in the West by sisterhoods or cloisters. Widows have been sent for special training in Colleges or Hospitals where they learn to be teachers or nurses.

Krupabai Satthianadhan elaborates with more detail on Ramabai's principles that were upheld by Nikambe. She maintained that the western learning which Ramabai's school provided did not 'corrupt' the traditional image of asceticism and selfless service but modified it in ways that erased the tragedy and stigma attached to Hindu widowhood, replacing it with tranquility. Although lengthy, I have the relevant extract from Satthianadhan's review, titled 'Pandita Ramabai and Her Work', as it vividly and comprehensively projects the image of the reformed Hindu widow, complementing Nikambe's own vision.

My first glimpse of the Pandita was quite startling. I expected to see an anglicized figure with a great deal of pomp and affectation about her, not without some repulsion on account of her great learning. But what was my surprise to see a figure neatly and quietly dressed in white in the regular Brahminic style, with a fair open countenance, beaming with intelligence, and with eyes keen and sparkling.... She came in quite naturally, shook hands and was ready to enter into conversation. Her self-possession struck me very much....

She had under training about forty widows, and referring to the opposition that she had to meet with from the orthodox party she said in a determined manner: 'I do not care what people say. If I had been guided by all that people say my work would have collapsed long ago.' After a little conversation she took us round to the various classes. One class was engaged in doing sums, one in reading and another in writing, and as we saw class after class were surprised to notice the keen intelligence shown by some of the pupils. They were of all ages and almost all of them were Brahmins.... I felt I could see in the downcast eyes and beaten down looks of some the hardships they must have undergone in their homes; but in all the faces now there was a glow of cheerfulness and relief which clearly showed that, whatever they might have suffered in the past, they were free and happy now, and they deeply enjoyed the freedom they were enjoying.... They seemed to have shaken off all prejudices and in the new atmosphere of freedom and intellectual development to have acquired some force of character and determination to improve themselves. Everything they do whether singing or reading or talking, they do naturally, without any of that false modesty and affectation which characterize Hindu girls of their age. How much fuller, brighter and healthier the life of our girls would be if they could only throw off the trammels of superstition and prejudice and breathe the healthy atmosphere of innocent enjoyment and culture! Pandita Ramabai's work is national in its effects, for the widows that she is training are sure to take the lead in the emancipation of women of India.[31]

At this point it would be interesting to compare briefly, Satthianadhan's novel *Kamala* and *Ratanbai*. Published within a year of each other, both deal with child-wives, and are obvious social novels. However, *Kamala* also incorporates specific features of the psychological novel. While Satthianadhan's primary purpose is reformatory, committed to the cause of female emancipation, images and situations described in the novel render the heroine in terms of her responsiveness as an individual, not simply a social type. Certain unique perceptions impinge on Kamala as she experiences a typical contemporary Hindu wife's life. These construct the inner structure of Kamala's psychology out of which emerges an identity that could be defined individualistically as well as archetypally.[32]

By contrast, *Ratanbai*, though intent on reform, displays a decisive difference. In this novel, in contrast to *Kamala*, the heroine's introspective psychological encounter with and response to external experience is never directly probed. Consequently, her inner-self is never analysed. There is hardly any reconciliation of the inner with the outer world. When it is even momentarily touched on, the writer generally assumes a detached viewpoint and describes Ratan's consciousness peripherally, through external events as in the following passage:

[31] Satthianadhan, 'Pandita Ramabai and her Work', in *Miscellaneous Writings* (Madras: Srinivasa, Varadachari and Co, 1896), pp. 94–5.

[32] For a more detailed discussion on this, see my introduction to *Kamala: The Story of a Hindu Wife* (First ed., New Delhi: Oxford University Press, 1998) or *Kamala: The Story of a Hindu Child-Wife* (Second ed., New Delhi: Oxford University Press, 2002).

...a sad feeling took hold of Ratanbai and she could not bear it any longer. She flung herself into her mother's lap, weeping most bitterly. She was such a darling in the house that the mother and the aunt could not endure to see her so troubled, and by caressing and coaxing, brought her to herself again.

...She soon went to her mother's side; and holding her sari she gave way to convulsive sobs and cries until her father took her near him and quietened her.

In *Kamala*, the author (at least occasionally) fearlessly exposes the full flood of Kamala's protest against the narrow confines of orthodoxy. In those moments, however fleeting, Kamala becomes the revolutionary, and through her inner conflict the writer articulates a new set of values for the Hindu woman. Even if she finally surrenders to tradition, she is made aware of choices. On the other hand, Ratan is consistently the ideal orthodox Hindu female prototype, shaped by dominant social norms for womanhood. She is never allowed a voice of her own or any agency. She responds to every crisis with a code of values that can only be described as feminine and in line with traditional role models of daughter and wife that have been imposed on her from infancy. The following passage conveys Ratan's reaction to the series of events that have reduced her education to a sporadic ineffective pastime, and in its negative emotion and ideological insinuation, typifies her manner of response to the tyranny of orthodoxy:

Ratan kept silent. She did feel so sorry, and the disappointment could be seen in her sad face. That evening she went upstairs to the top room and cried herself to sleep. She refused to rise and have supper, and when her mother went to her she simply wept.

This is a rebellion that is altogether passive; Nikambe grants her heroine no articulate demands for self-development. When Ratan's education is repeatedly interrupted by the demands of role-indoctrination such as pilgrimages, domestic training, and visits to relatives, she acquiesces, and even takes each of these substitutes for education in her stride. This response is certainly realistic in that the Hindu code of life inhibits individual choice and personal protest. Ratan endures and accepts her own confinement, no matter how stifling it may be; she acquiesces in her own deprivation.

The restrained characterization of Ratan is significant, and throws light on the framework within which the author functioned. Like her fictional counterpart in the novel, Vasudevrav, she was transformed by western ideologies and education. Like him, she protests against the constraints of orthodoxy, and attempts reform by introducing liberal ideologies. In her persona as reformer, she involves Ratan in typical contemporary situations that threaten Ratan's education in order to expose traditional inhibitions and reactions against it. Whenever Ratan's education is neglected or terminated, she highlights it as both irresponsible and ignorant behaviour, through Kaku and Ratan's in-laws. However, as discussed, she lamely resorts (like Vasudevrav) to plot machination rather than to the free choice of her characters, to attain her objective of educating Ratan.

Nikambe's reluctance to portray conflict or self-assertion in Ratan is, in all probability, linked to the social realities of the woman writer in a patriarchal culture. Satthianadhan, who belonged to a 'reformed' family of Christian converts and married an Indian-Christian with similar liberal views, had the license to criticize restrictive patriarchal conventions that frustrated the self-development of the orthodox Hindu woman. She also inaugurated a school for Muslim girls under the auspices of the CMS Mission, and was actively involved in Christian missionary work in the zenanas. At the time of writing *Ratanbai*, Nikambe was the headmistress of a high-caste Hindu girls' school. A significant segment of her readership could have comprised her students and their parents. These factors suggest that the school authorities had to accommodate the pressures of orthodox ideology if they were to impart a more challenging education to its students, as intimated by Lady Harris in her Preface to *Ratanbai*. The pressure of ideology and its accommodation are effectively adduced in the novel through the incident where Ratan spends an evening at a party organized by a female British patron to her school. Here, the author makes a special attempt to create a respectable occasion when the western lifestyle can be introduced to the students without offence, and without damage to their own particular code of values. At this party, the hostess, the representative of the West, is seen to conform readily to the conventions of Brahmins, a sect of the caste to which Ratan belongs. The meal has been cooked and served by Brahmins. When Ratan carefully imparts this fact to her mother and to Kaku, their anxiety that Ratan has been exposed to pollution by the visit is slightly pacified.

In the light of the above evidence, it is possible to conclude that Nikambe had to resort to self-imposed restraints if *Ratanbai* was to reach its intended audience as an effective weapon in women's emancipation. This strategy has interesting parallels in many eighteenth- and nineteenth-century novels that dealt with feminine conduct. They were novels structured around childhood initiation, bent on 'inculcating the norms of womanhood into young readers, mixing fiction with prescription in a manner that fascinated them while pleasing their parents'.[33] Like the protagonists of these novels, as for example, Fanny Fern's six-year-old Rose and Martha Finley's Elsie, Ratan is subjected by her author to sadism and suffering (in the sasar's house) but although this makes her sad, she is shown to bow to authority in the sweetest manner possible, 'respectful to superiors and kind to inferiors and equals, gentle, sweet-tempered, patient, and forgiving to a remarkable degree'. Claims could thus be advanced to situate *Ratanbai* generally within a female literary movement, international in scope.

Other complexities emerge on close examination. For instance, there seems to be, in the writer's exposure of Ratan's prototypical response to society's demands on her, only a surface acceptance, an acceptance that secretly denotes what Patricia Meyer Spacks has termed 'subterranean challenges' in women's fiction.[34] Ratan's mute acceptance of her fate can be seen to underscore the helplessness of the female situation that seems in dire need of reformation. A distinctive feature of this novel, then, is 'that presence of absence' discernible in some literature

---

[33] For a detailed discussion see Pratt, *Archetypal Patterns*, pp. 15–16.

[34] Patricia Meyer Spacks, *The Female Imagination: A Literary and Psychological Investigation of Women's Writing* (London: George Allen and Unwin, 1976), p. 317.

by women, 'the hollows, centers, caverns within the work—places where activity that one might expect is missing...or deceptively coded'.[35] It is in these areas of fictional experience that the borders between the social and psychological novel subtly blur and cross. The following passage that describes Ratan's debut in the novel is a case in point:

> One morning, as Mr Vasudevrav is busy with his clients, little Ratanbai, a pet with her father, walks in, and, *carrying a chair to the window, kneels on it and looks out on the road*. She is dressed, as all Hindu girls are, in a skirt of the *khan* [Hindu ladies' cloth] material, and a short-sleeved satin jacket. Her tiny fair wrists are covered with gold bracelets, six on each, with a couple of gold stone bangles between. Round her neck is a *mangalsutra* [wedding symbol: a necklace], a *sa-ri* [a heavy gold neck ornament], a *goph*. Her ears have diamond and pearl earrings. Her hair is parted in the middle, brushed, well oiled, and tied into a neat knot at the back. Upon this knot she wears a brooch-like jewel, over which a *veni* [a wreath of flowers] is fixed. Her skirt reaches her ankles; but as she kneels, it is a bit untidy and one can see her pretty grape-patterned anklets. Two toes, the first and the third, have silver rings. Ratanbai *stayed at the window for a few moments, then getting off the chair, she stood by the table, watching her learned father* as he dictated to half a dozen clerks who squatted on the floor and scribbled away with reed pens. She looked charming. Her fair complexion made her to be classed amongst the pretty girls of Bombay. As she stood in a careless dreamy way looking at the flying pens of the clerks, her kind father's attention was towards her... [italics mine]

A superficial reading of this passage would see Ratan introduced as the archetypal high-caste Hindu girl for Nikambe's local readership (students and parents), while the exoticization of her dress would be construed as having been provided for the benefit of readers unfamiliar with such cultural niceties. It seems to express even the author's endorsement of this archetype, attired in traditional dress, demure and feminine. However, the author's apparent support of this orthodox ideology is accompanied by subversive resistance to it. Ratan's physical attributes (as, for example, her 'tiny fair wrist' and 'fair complexion') are emphasized as attributes of femininity. Considered from an

---

[35] Carolyn Heilbrun and Catherine Slimpson as cited in Gilbert and Gubar, *The Madwoman in the Attic: The Woman Writer and the Nineteenth Century* (London: Yale University Press, 1980), p. 84.

alternative point of view, however, Ratan's dress, covering every inch of her body, and the heavy ornaments with which she is decorated, comprise an imagery of entrapment, and as such serve as a leitmotif common to the general women's Bildungsroman: psychical imprisonment. Dress and festivals in this fiction have been seen by Gilbert and Gubar as really the paraphernalia of confinement; instruments that indicate imprisonment.[36] While ornaments have perennially decorated Hindu males and females, it is relevant, at this juncture, to highlight their symbolic significance to the female person. An unidentified but informative source provides an insight into the symbolic meanings ascribed to the traditional Hindu bridal jewellery that has adorned many aristocratic brides. This source maintains that the jewellery was meant symbolically to reinforce a code of feminine behaviour that inevitably limited the woman's freedom of thought and action:

A *tikka* for the forehead, worn in the parting of the hair, signifying 'walk on the straight path', earrings to remind you not to have weak ears and listen to gossip, a necklace so that your head is always bowed down in humility, bangles to tell you that your hand must always go forward for giving charity and anklets so that you put the right foot forward—and the nose-ring of which it was said that the pearl should not be heavier than the nose, meaning you should not spend more than what your husband could afford. So every bride was given these and told the significance and she had to wear them throughout her married life.[37]

Whether intended deliberately or not, Nikambe's portrait of Ratan (above) is imbued with similar psychological symbolism.

There are other seemingly innocent moments in the novel that symbolically unveil layers of meaning. Interestingly, Ratan's intellectual liberation always occurs on male territory (as in the above extract), primarily in the domain of her father. At the same time, readers might note the significance of the only two actions mentioned in the previous extract from *Ratanbai* (italicized) which otherwise deals passively with clothes and

[36] Gilbert and Gubar, *The Madwoman in the Attic*, p. 84.
[37] Charles Allen and Sharada Dwivedi, *Lives of the Indian Princes* (London: Arrow, 1984), p. 132.

ornaments. While Ratan is a docile Brahmin girl, each action described in the passage could be seen to suggest her inarticulated desire (awakened by education) to experience life outside the confines of home, a life as yet out of reach. The road could suggest freedom just as the pen symbolizes knowledge. In *The Story of an African Farm*, published in 1883, Olive Schreiner depicts a similar situation: her heroine's aspirations for liberation are frustrated, like Ratan's, by repressive gender norms, and the heroine is taught early in life that a woman's most significant asset in the quest for a 'successful' life was not intellectuality but physical beauty:

'Look at this little chin of mine, Waldo, with the dimple in it. It is but a small part of my person; but though I had a knowledge of all things under the sun, and the wisdom to use it, and the deep loving heart of an angel, it would not stead me through life like this little chin. I can win money with it, I can win love; I can win power with it, I can win fame. What would knowledge help me? The less a woman has in her head the lighter she is for climbing. I once heard an old man say, that he never saw an intellect help a woman so much as a pretty ankle; and it was the truth. They begin to shape us to our cursed end,' she said, with her lips drawn in to look as though they smiled, 'when we are tiny things in shoes and socks. We sit with our little feet drawn up under us in the window, and look out at the boys in their happy play. We want to go. Then a loving hand is laid on us: "little one you cannot go," they say; "Your little face will burn, and your nice white dress will be spoilt." We feel it must be for our good it is so lovingly said but we cannot understand; and we kneel still with our little cheek wistfully pressed against the pane. Afterwards we go and thread blue beads, and make a string for our neck; and we go and stand before the glass. We see the complexion we were not to spoil, and the white frock, and we look into our own great eyes.'[38]

The main difference between this passage and the previous extract from *Ratanbai* lies in the way each writer addresses her respective readership. Posing as a male writer under the *nom-de-plume* Ralph Iron, Schreiner could safely give vent to her anger against gender norms and female injustice; not so a Hindu woman addressing under her own name a readership entrenched in tradition.

[38] Olive Schreiner, *The Story of an African Farm* (1883; rpt. Harmondsworth, Middlesex: Penguin, 1971), p. 189.

Nikambe's presentation of the marriage ceremony of Ratan and Prataprao is a further illustration of the ways in which she surmounts her inhibitions. The exchange of verses that takes place between Ratan and her husband at their marriage ceremony, and the actions that accompany this exchange seem inserted in the novel merely for the purpose of informing the foreign segment of her readership about Indian customs. Yet, they also suggest the totally different roles that gender norms designate for the male and female, the inequities in power that exist between a husband and wife. The verses imply that marriage is not a merging of equals but rests on the subordination of the woman to the man. The husband is seen to 'allow' his wife to wash his feet, to dry them, and to garland him. Her actions acknowledge his superiority while her words stress her acceptance that his main function in life is to gain glory and fame in public life. The husband, on the other hand, merely presents his wife with a wreath of flowers, an ornament for her hair symbolic of one function of the wife—of being an adornment. His words underline a serious threat: the wife must make no blunders in good or in bad times; she must set a good example to all. The status signified by the title 'queen', is nullified by the conditions and warning attached to it.

Nikambe's method of conveying controversial feminist views to a traditional and male-dominated society, which gives an unexpected dimension of subversive meaning to her novel, places her once more in a literary tradition to which some of her western contemporary sister writers—confronting similar conditions—belonged. Like them, she also protests not by directly confronting the cause but by seeming to conform to it, by 'voicing their objections while they drown out [its] effect'.[39] Other authorities on women's literature, like Gilbert and Gubar address the same phenomenon and analyse techniques alluded to by Annis Pratt above. A particular technique described by Gilbert and Gubar has close parallels with

---

[39] Pratt, *Archetypal Patterns*, p. 15.

Introduction xli

the strategy of implication used by Nikambe in her novel to address tactfully a controversial subject:

> In effect, such women [successful women writers of the nineteenth century] have created submerged meanings, meanings hidden within or behind the more accessible, 'public' content of their works, so that their literature could be read and appreciated even when its vital concern with female dispossession and disease was ignored.
>
> ...[W]hile they achieve essential authority by telling their own stories, these writers allay their distinctively female anxieties of authorship by following Emily Dickinson's famous [characteristic] advice to 'Tell the truth but tell it slant'. In short, women from Jane Austen and Mary Shelley to Emily Brontë and Emily Dickinson produced literary works that are in some sense palimpsestic, works whose surface designs conceal or obscure deeper, less accessible (and less socially acceptable) levels of meaning. Thus these authors managed the difficult task of achieving true female literary authority by simultaneously conforming to and subverting patriarchal literary standards.

Thus, it can be concluded that *Ratanbai*, a seemingly simple and unassuming novel, can be appreciated at different levels of meaning. Read in its time by the particular readership to which it was addressed, the novel could be seen as promoting education for girls, young wives, and widows in an instructive and culturally acceptable manner. It would certainly have pleased even the most rigid of her readers like the 'revivalist nationalist' political group that emerged in the last decades of the nineteenth century, who believed in the preservation of the Hindu tradition and patriarchy in the face of colonialist reform.[40] Read more than a century later, it can be interpreted as a subversively rebellious socio-psychological novel inspired by the nineteenth-century woman writer's main source of inspiration—the female consciousness alive to change, striving for liberation from the restriction and tyranny of entrenched convention reinforced by reactionary ideology.

Chandani Lokugé

[40] See Tanika Sarkar, 'Colonial Lawmaking and Lives/Deaths of Indian Women: Different Readings of Law and Community' in Ratna Kapur (ed.), *Feminist Terrains in Legal Domains: Interdisciplinary Essays on Women and Law in India* (New Delhi: Kali for Women, 1996).

RATANBAI

*By Special permission most graciously accorded,
This Book is Dedicated
with profound gratitude and loyalty*

TO

HER MOST GRACIOUS MAJESTY THE QUEEN,
EMPRESS OF INDIA

BY

SHEVANTIBAI M. NIKAMBE

CONTENTS

Preface by Her Excellency The Lady Harris, C.I.	7
Preface by Shevantibai M. Nikambe	9
Chapter 1	11
Chapter 2	23
Chapter 3	32
Chapter 4	45

PREFACE BY
HER EXCELLENCY THE LADY HARRIS, C.I.

I have much pleasure in writing these few lines, and feel sure that the readers of this Hindu story will be interested to hear that the authoress is the head of a Hindu school for high-caste girls, and therefore has had every opportunity for studying their characteristics.

The school is of immense help to her country-women, who are, as a rule, prevented from being properly trained in sometimes even the simplest forms of education by their high caste and their early marriages, which, as a rule, prevent girls from going to school after twelve years of age—the very time when our English girls are beginning to see more clearly the advantages of education. A married Hindu lady naturally does not like to go to big native schools: it being undignified in their ideas to learn with girls, perhaps of not such high caste as their own, or else unmarried.

Mrs Nikambe's school was started in November 1890 with five pupils. Before she opened this school, she was engaged in educational work amongst the high-caste girls and women in Bombay: she was the headmistress of a Hindu girls' school in connexion with the well-known and influential society called the 'Students' Literary and Scientific Society'. She saw the disadvantages and difficulties the little Hindu wives had in getting a decent education after they were married.

Ever since her school has been started, the young wives, widows, and grown-up girls of the high-caste community have taken advantage of it. Young mothers have come, too.

I have myself visited Mrs Nikambe's school—a visit that gave me great pleasure; and I was charmed with what I saw and heard, and think Mrs Nikambe worthy of all praise for carrying on with so much earnestness a greatly needed work.

I feel sure that all married Hindu ladies must be happier and better for an education which, whilst not too engrossing, must be elevating to themselves, their children, and homes.

Ada Harris

PREFACE

In placing this humble work before the public (my very first attempt), I have to thank and praise God with all my heart for help and strength, especially in my late illness, during which time it was written.

I feel I must record my deep indebtedness to Her Gracious Majesty the Queen, our beloved Empress, for so graciously granting me the permission to dedicate this small work to Her Majesty, whose happy rule in my dear native land is brightening and enlightening the lives and homes of many Hindu women.

My warmest thanks are due to Her Excellency the Lady Harris, C.I., the wife of the late Governor of Bombay, for her deep interest in India's women, and for so kindly writing the preface to this book. I have also to thank Miss Manning for looking over the proofs and suggesting corrections.

Shevantibai M. Nikambe

London, June 1895

CHAPTER I

Young Ratanbai is a pleasing girl of eleven. Her father's name is Vasudevrav Kashinath Dalvi, and her mother's Anandibai. Mr Vasudevrav is a successful lawyer of the High Court. Every morning he is busy with his clients in the office room, which is very comfortably furnished. A rich carpet covers the floor; a cushioned sofa stands at one side, a dozen chairs in a row at the other, a handsome cabinet containing a large collection of law books opposite, and there are two good windows looking to the front. The walls are prettily decorated, and portraits of great men, mostly literary, hang in a most uncomfortable fashion high up against the roof. Mr Vasudevrav likes his home to be well furnished, and once in a while he does give his spare time to this matter; but generally he only makes the purchases and sends them home, leaving all to his clerk Narayanrao, who, though a clever and an honest man, knows little about making a room attractive.

One morning, as Mr Vasudavrav is busy with his clients, little Ratanbai, a pet with her father, walks in, and, carrying a chair to the window, kneels on it and looks out on the road. She is dressed, as all Hindu girls are, in a skirt of the *khan*[1] material, and a short-sleeved satin jacket. Her tiny fair wrists are covered with gold bracelets, six on each, with a couple of gold stone

---

[1] The Hindu ladies' cloth.

bangles between. Round her neck is a *mangalsutra*,[2] a *sa-ri*,[3] a *goph*.[4] Her ears have diamond and pearl earrings. Her hair is parted in the middle, brushed, well oiled, and tied into a neat knot at the back. Upon this knot she wears a brooch-like jewel, over which a *veni*[5] is fixed. Her skirt reaches her ankles; but as she kneels, it is a bit untidy, and one can see her pretty grape-patterned anklets. Two toes, the first and the third, have silver rings. Ratanbai stayed at the window for a few moments, then getting off the chair, she stood by the table, watching her learned father as he dictated to half a dozen clerks who squatted on the floor and scribbled away with reed pens. She looked charming. Her fair complexion made her to be classed amongst the pretty girls of Bombay. As she stood in a careless dreamy way, looking at the flying pens of the clerks, her kind father's attention was turned towards her, and thoughts seemed to crowd into his head while he stretched lazily on his chair. Then coming to himself, and putting his velvet cap straight, he again attended to his work. No one knew what filled his mind with care, and child Ratan did not notice her father at all. She little knew the anxiety her good parent had had ever since her marriage.

Ratanbai had been married two years before into a wealthy but uneducated family. The promise was made by the mother with the father's consent, when the girl was a baby, and the arrangement had to be fulfilled, though it had been against the real wish of the educated father. Unfortunately, four months after the marriage, her father-in-law, Harischandra Sadashiva, successful merchant and a wealthy landowner, died, and his widow, according to the rules of the caste had to live under the shelter of her husband's brother, who was rich, but not very pleasant to deal with. His wife, who belonged to the country, was ignorant, and always made matters worse through sheer want of education. Ratanbai's mother-in-law, then, was in great

[2] The wedding symbol. It is a necklace of small black beads, with a pretty gold ornament in the middle.
[3] A heavy gold neck ornament.
[4] A beautiful woven ornament of fine real gold strings. It fits round the neck.
[5] A wreath of flowers.

trouble, and Mr Vasudevrav became at times full of grief, for it was clear that Ratan's young husband, who was pursuing his studies at college, would soon be obliged to take up the management of the affairs, and this would indeed come in the way of his studies. Such a necessity was a great disappointment to Mr Vasudevrav, whose great aim was to have as his son-in-law a learned man, and, if possible, one who would be a lawyer. Every time he looked at Ratanbai, his only surviving and therefore darling child, anxiety filled his mind.

In about half-an-hour, Mr Vasudevrav was at breakfast. The dining room was dismal looking, with only a dozen low flat stools to boast of as furniture. It was, however, very clean, and we will mention the details of the meal.

Mr Vasudevrav seats himself on one of the stools, before which is a large silver *tat*,[6] a *vati*,[7] a silver water jug, and cup. He is dressed in a rich maroon *mughta*.[8] The upper part of his body is bare, the sacred thread hangs across his shoulder; a gold ornament, like a handsome bracelet, is tightly fixed above his elbow, and a pearl earring is in the upper part of his ear. His head is shaved, except at the back, whence hang curly jet tresses. He is a tall, fine-looking man. As soon as he sits down, his wife, Anandibai, gently and modestly steps in, and sitting on the floor pours a little water into the plate, and running her fingers through, throws the water into a corner nearby, when a cup full of rice is laid in it by the cook with *varana*[9] over it. Anandibai brings in a *vati* of butter, and pours a couple of teaspoonfuls over the rice. In the meantime, the *polli*,[10] the vegetables, and the pickles, and sweets and fruits are served, and Mr Vasudevrav, alone and in silence, devours his fresh hot breakfast. Sometimes he asks for more of some dish which Anandibai serves. He tries some more rice,

---

[6] A large plate.
[7] A cup.
[8] The habit worn by gentlemen when dining.
[9] A preparation of a kind of pulse always used with rice.
[10] Cake or scone.

with milk and home-made curds, and, finishing the sweets and the fruits, draws a bright-polished brass basin closer, washes his hands, and looks for a napkin, which his good wife hands to him. He now walks straight up to his room to dress, which operation takes very little time, for everything is lying ready, and a servant is present to help in the way of drawing on the boots, etc.

In the meantime Ratanbai had had her breakfast, and was ready also. The carriage—a handsome landau, drawn by a pair of fine white horses, a gift from one of the clients—came to the door. Mr Vasudevrav, who is dressed in a long white coat and trousers, with a handsome red turban, gets in first, and little Ratanbai seats herself opposite him. With two footmen at the back of the carriage, and a messenger by the coachman's side, they drive through the crowded, busy streets. After ten minutes the carriage stopped. One of the footmen not in a livery jumped down, and helping Ratanbai out, walked behind her with her bag of school books into a large broad stone house, and placing the bag in its place, left Ratanbai among her friends, saying loudly before leaving, "Ratanbai, please be ready; I have been told to come for you at two o'clock today, so I will bring your milk and then take you home." At this Ratanbai looked at him and simply nodded her head. The carriage in the meantime drove on to the High Court, and the servant, after seeing Ratanbai at school, made calls on his friends, and had a short smoke and nap before returning home.

The bell rang and the girls went into their respective classrooms. Let us go into the III. Standard Class. It is upstairs, and we must ascend the broad staircase. The room is well ventilated and suitably furnished. There are twelve girls in the class, all young wives. Three are dressed in the *sari*, and the rest like Ratanbai. At the head of the class is our friend Ratanbai, looking intelligent and modest as she stands up to read the third verse of *Casabianca*. She reads it distinctly, with expression, as if she understood every word, and then she follows the next reader by looking into her book. A visitor might at once perceive how well behaved and good Ratanbai is at school. She never joins in any sort of mischief, is never found inattentive, in fact, she is, as her teacher is delighted to say, "the nicest girl that attends our school".

At one o'clock the servant brought her tiffin—milk and cake; the former in a silver cup, and the latter in a silver basket. Ratanbai did not go out of the class when her servant arrived, as some of the girls did, but she waited until the "recess hour"; then she went quietly into the tiffin room, seated herself on the floor, and drank the milk first and then ate the cake. After washing her hands at the pipe in the outer room, she ran upstairs to her teacher, ascertained her lessons for the next day, then bidding goodbye in her sweet way, with a smile and a gentle nod of the head, putting on her *shalu*,[11] she walked out, the servant again behind her with her bag, and drove home.

Anandibai, her mother, was at her toilet. She was seated on the floor before a looking glass, with caskets of jewellery near, and was just taking a pair of pearl studs out of her ear, when Ratan ran in and embraced her.

"Go to Gangu," said the mother, "and she will do your hair, and then I want you to wear your *pilav*[12] to-day. We are to go to *Mavashi's phule*."[13]

By four o'clock the mother and the daughter were dressed, and the brougham was at the door. Ratanbai wore a light blue *pilav* with gold trimming. Her jacket was of pink satin, most elaborately worked with gold thread and pearls. She had on a set of pearl jewellery, and wore a handsome nose ring. Gracefully raising the edge of her dress, she jumped into the carriage; her mother, who was very neatly attired, follows, and with two attendants they drove through the bustling streets into one of the newly built stone bungalows in Ghaum. As they neared the house, they heard the *vajantri*,[14] or tom-tom. Anandibai and Ratan got out, and were led into the hall, which was most

---

[11] A silk shawl with gold thread.
[12] A silk sari—like the Parsi.
[13] The flower ceremony of the maternal aunt.
[14] The native band.

grandly arranged. The chairs, sofas, and tables were moved into another room; a rich carpet spread, the chandeliers and wall lamps were uncovered and lit. The Hindu ladies dressed all alike, but in variegated colours, were seated in groups on the carpet. Some were talking, some helping themselves to *pan supari*,[15] and some putting flowers in their hair. There were about a hundred in the room, and yet the entrance was crowded. The ladies looked very dignified as they entered, dressed in different kinds of *saris*, with handsome-coloured cashmere shawls thrown over their shoulders. Each meets the hostess, then takes a seat amidst the crowd, and looks round about at the house, etc., and is soon lost in talk. Anandibai and Ratanbai, being the nearest relatives, go into the inner room first, and then into the outer hall.

Anandibai's youngest sister, Champubai, is married into this house. She is a lovely girl of fourteen, and it is on her account that this festivity takes place. In about an hour, Champubai, most gorgeously dressed in the handsomest silk and gold, and with abundant jewellery, walks into the room, when every eye is turned to her. She takes her seat in the lovely pandal, especially put up for the occasion—on a velvet-cushioned chair—and, placing her jewelled feet on a low stool, she sits, a picture of perfect beauty. The oval face, the light olive complexion, the lovely black expressive eyes, the chiselled nose, and the small mouth, all go to make Champubai one of the beauties of Bombay. Her luxuriant jet-black hair is hung in a plait decorated with flowers of the sweetest scent; an artistic net of jasmine buds covers her head, and her forehead from ear to ear is edged by a piece of pearl lace, and an ornament of about the size of a shilling is suspended by a pearl string at the parting. Her ears are masses of beautiful pearls and diamonds, and so are the arms and the neck. The *pilav* she wears is of a soft pink, and worked all over with gold. Her delicate feet have ornaments like Ratanbai's, only these are larger. The pandal is against a large handsome mirror, and is like a fairy bower, arranged with plants, and lamps, and candles. At

---

[15] The leaves and the betel nut—offered to guests as a symbol of the hospitality of Hindus.

the side of Champubai are two dais, which are occupied by young girls dressed gracefully; amongst them, to the right hand is little Ratanbai.

The ladies of the house are in a state of confusion and bustle. There are so many duties to be carried out, but no arrangement had been made beforehand as to who would perform them. Finally, the hostess tells one to go to the distribution of coconuts, two to the serving of spiced milk, one to distribute the flowers, another to attend to the *pan supari*; while she herself attends to her daughter-in-law. She carries a silver tray with the following articles in it: a little rice, a tiny box of *kunku*,[16] and a small lamp, and places the tray at the feet of Champubai. Holding the lamp up to Champubai's face, she waves it in the usual way, and putting a promissory note of Rs 50 in her daughter-in-law's hand, places the lamp in the tray and applies the *kunku* and rice between the eyebrows, extending this last ceremony to Ratanbai and the other little girls.

After this an unusual noise prevails, and much confusion follows in distributing the sweets and serving the milk; the last is done in another room, the ladies going in groups of ten or twelve. A little after lamplight all is over, yet the poorer and older women of the caste keep on coming, if not to witness the ceremony, at least to receive sweets and coconuts. Anandibai and Ratanbai are urged to take dinner, which they do hurriedly, for Anandibai is anxious to get home to her husband. To her surprise and Ratan's pleasure, Mr Vasudevrav calls for them in the carriage before proceeding home. The gentlemen of the house, however, urge him to get out and remain a while, which he does. He is led into the drawing room, and the hospitality of *pan supari* is offered. After some jokes they begin to talk on the topics of the day, and so engrossed was Mr Vasudevrav in the conversation that Anandibai goes home alone with Ratanbai and sends the carriage back for her husband.

For a whole week Champubai was engaged in this way with ceremonies, and each day she was dressed in a different way. One

---

[16] The red paste or powder with which the ladies make the dot on the forehead.

day like a *bhatin*,[17] the second day like a *vanin*,[18] the third day like a parsi lady, and so on, and all these days Ratanbai is kept away from school. Finally her mother pronounces there are no more festivities, and that Ratan can attend school. But the next day a message comes from the mother-in-law that she was required there for a certain ceremony at her husband's sister's house. To her mother-in-law's then she went for a week. Ratanbai never liked going to *sasar*,[19] for she was not allowed any freedom there. She had always to be helping with something or other, and to be in complete subjection to everyone. She could not take her school possessions to that house, for it was her mother-in-law's sister-in-law who was the ruling person in the home, and she was already educated in the old style, and was most averse to "new or reformed ideas". Ratanbai's mother-in-law was nobody there. So Ratanbai dared not carry a lesson book into that home, and the consequence was that the bright happy child was turned into a miserable girl for a week. Sitting idly for hours, helping to clean the vegetables and grain, gossiping with the neighbouring girls of her age, listening to all sorts of talk of the elderly women were the usual occupations of Ratanbai at the *sasar*. She could not feel happy in this cheerless life. All the members of the family were a terror to the child. From the day she arrived to the day she left all kinds of remarks would be made, and especially remarks that hurt her. Something about her father and mother, about being sent to school and being *learned*, was constantly falling on her ears. Yet she did not say a word, did not show signs of unpleasantness. Her duty was to please, and to be most obedient. How often she thought of the school, and the companions and the teachers, and longed to be amongst them! But as a married girl her lot was first of all with her husband's people. Very likely if her father-in-law had been alive, her mother-in-law would have removed her from school after her tenth birthday, but to please Ratan's father she was very quiet.

---

[17] A term used by the Gaud Brahmins for the Brahmin lady.
[18] Bania lady.
[19] The father-in-law's house.

At last the day for her returning to her parents arrived, and Ratan longed to fly as a bird; but, no! she must wait till she is sent for. The carriage, after taking the gentlemen to the office and the college, came back, and with the permission of her mother-in-law, she went back to her parents. How pleased she was to be again at her dear home! Now she might fly from one room to another, and be petted and caressed by all, a little queen among the servants. The silent patient *suna*[20] became again a free bright happy child. The unkind words that had been uttered, the harsh way in which she has been treated, she dared not mention to her mother or fond father, for telling them would only make matters worse. The mother-in-law and others connected would simply have shown themselves more tyrannical. First, when Ratanbai began her visits to her *sasar*, she would cry, and tell her parents of these unkind manners, but that made her parents grieve, and if they ventured to speak about it even in a right way it simply went badly for Ratanbai, so though she felt all this very keenly, she bore it silently and dutifully.

The day she returned to her parents her first duty was to attend to her lessons. Asking the servant to bring her bag, she took it into her father's office, and, seated on the floor, opened it, taking out all the books one by one, carefully examined them. After giving the books and other articles a thorough airing, she replaced them neatly, keeping, however, one book out. This she opened and read, learning her poetry and spelling by heart. Then, taking her home exercise book, she wrote out her exercises on her father's desk, using his ink and pen. Her heart was happy at the thought of going to school the next day.

Whenever Ratanbai was at home Anandibai was very regular in getting the wreaths, and Ratanbai had one put in her hair. Her mother that afternoon made a call, and Ratanbai was allowed to accompany her. Before lamplight they returned, and while Anandibai was busily occupied in household duties, Ratanbai took out a piece of needlework, and in the office room awaited

---

[20] Daughter-in-law.

the return of her father. She merrily hummed one of the infant school tunes, and was then singing softly a Sanskrit *shloka*, when the sound of the carriage was heard, and Ratanbai, flinging down her work, ran to the window, but to her disappointment, instead of the carriage with her father in it she saw a hack victoria with a load of luggage. Two months ago, an old widowed aunt of Ratanbai's father had gone on a pilgrimage to Benares. Mr Vasudevrav had provided her with attendants, etc., and the arrival of this victoria means that the old lady had returned. The servants crowded to take the luggage, and then the old lady was helped out. She was dressed in pure white, and covered from the head to a little above her ankles. Her head was shaved, and the *patal*[21] so carefully covered it that you could only see her tired face, which in its day had been attractive. Embracing Ratanbai and her mother, she pronounced her blessing, and sat down in a wearied fashion. Anandibai and Ratanbai sit beside her, and ask as to what kind of a journey she had, whether the train was crowded, and how many were returning from the pilgrimage, etc. Each question received a lengthy answer, and the attendants here and there helped to make the replies still more lengthy.

After a while Anandibai rose and walked towards the kitchen, and the old lady, understanding that it was to give an order for her supper, said: "Do not trouble. I will just take milk."

"Kakubai," says Ratanbai's mother, "you will have a little rice, surely?"

"Well, if it is hot; but do not cook any fresh for me."

"Oh, it will be no trouble, for we have not dined yet."

"What, not dined! Vasudevrav is not at home yet, I suppose?"

"No; *Baba*[22] must be at the club today," said Ratanbai.

The old lady here rose, and carrying a bundle from amongst the luggage to where Ratanbai sat, opened it, and took up several bags and gave them to her. Rejoicing over them, she exclaimed, "Kaku, have you brought all these for me?"

"Yes, birdie, they are for you," said the auntie, pinching Ratan's chin.

[21] A white sari.
[22] Father.

The creaking sound of the English boots announced Mr Vasudevrav's return home. He had been to a lecture in the "Hindu Club". The *bhaya*[23] at the door stands up and says, "*Sheth, Kakubai aye hai.*"[24] With feelings of pleasure and astonishment he entered the house, and found Kakubai and Ratanbai sitting together. After exchanging greetings, they talked for a while, when it was announced that "dinner is served". Mr Vasudevrav takes a few minutes to wash and dress, and is in his old seat; Anandibai is helping in the serving. As usual they sat talking after dinner, and Kakubai gave a long account of her pilgrimage, so that they all, even Ratanbai, retired at a late hour.

For two weeks Ratanbai is now able to go regularly to school. Every evening she might be seen sitting beside Kakubai, relating the day's incidents, and giving an enthusiastic account of the happy hours spent with the *Bai*[25] and the teachers in the girls' school.

---

[23] Caretaker.
[24] Sir, Kakubai has come.
[25] Mistress.

22   *Ratanbai*

A *Shenvi* Brahmin girl
A pupil in Mrs Nikambe's school
(Copyright The British Library)

CHAPTER II

One evening, Ratanbai was sitting beside her mother and Kakubai sewing, when the latter asked whether Shamrav's daughter had returned from Goa. Shamrav was a distant relative, and his daughter was attending the same school as Ratanbai.

Ratanbai: Yes; for she came to see *Bai*[1] yesterday, with Muktabai, her younger sister.

Kakubai: Both the girls are grown up now, and the father-in-law will remove them from school.

Ratanbai: We heard last week that Nanibai (Shamrav's elder girl) was not coming to school any more; but Nanibai told me yesterday that her mother-in-law has allowed her six months more, so she will be in school until *Divali*.[2]

Kakubai: Is Muktabai to go to school?

Ratanbai: Yes; she is coming also. Her husband is going up for the BA this year. If he passes, he intends trying for the LLB; but if he fails in that, he must get an appointment, and then probably, Muktabai will have to leave school. In our school there are five who intend going up for the matriculation examination, and one of them is Ghanashampant's daughter—Krishnabai.

Kakubai and Anandibai were very much astonished, and the former exclaimed, "What! Going up for men's examinations! What good are we to get by educating these girls?"

[1] School-mistress.
[2] The Hindu festival of lights.

"With all this education and examination they must 'bake the bread'," said the old aunt; and, turning to Ratanbai, she added, "What are you going to do by learning? Are you girls going to business now, and will you ask your husbands to mind the home?"

Anandibai: I do not think Ratanbai ought to go to school any longer, but her father wishes it, and I cannot go against his wish or decision.

Kakubai: How is her mother-in-law inclined towards it?

Anandibai: She has very little to say in the matter; and since Ratan's father-in-law's death, she does not behave as kindly as before, but of course her grief is overwhelming.

Kakubai (turning to Ratan): When you are at *sasar* does your mother-in-law send you to school?

"No," said Ratanbai, unwillingly.

Kakubai: Then why do you send her to school here, Anandi? Does Vasudev know of this?

"I think so," said Ratan's mother, "but there has been some understanding between Ratan's father and the mother-in-law."

While this talk was going on, a sad feeling took hold of Ratanbai, and she could not bear it any longer. She flung herself into her mother's lap, weeping most bitterly. She was such a darling in the house that the mother and the aunt could not endure to see her so troubled, and by caressing and coaxing, brought her to herself again. As she went away to wash her eyes, Anandibai whispered to Kakubai, "She cannot bear the idea of leaving school."

"I do not know what in the world you are going to get by educating her," remarked the old lady.

"I admit there is no good to be got, but it is Ratan's father's doing," replied Anandibai.

"I will talk to him tonight and see," said the old lady.

Anandibai went into the kitchen for a moment, and Kakubai sat in silent meditation.

Just as Anandibai came back, the servant walked in with a letter. "Keep it on the office table, *Bhaya*," said Anandibai to him.

"*Bai Saheb*, it is a telegram," answered the *Bhaya*.

At this they were both startled, and Kakubai exclaimed, "Why is there a telegram? Where does it come from, and from whom?" They took it in their hands and turned it upside down, and looked it well over; the letters and the address were like Greek to them; they could not make out anything.

"*Bhaya*, is the postman standing outside? Ask him where it is from," said Kakubai.

"He has gone," said *Bhaya*.

The whole household was in a state of excitement and confusion, but within half-an-hour, to their relief, the wheels of the carriage were heard, and Mr Vasudevrav appeared. The telegram was at once handed to him. He opened it and read, "Brother dangerously ill, come immediately." His face turned pale and he looked at his watch. It was half past eight. Kakubai and Anandibai ventured to come out and asked what was the matter.

"Dinnanath is ill, and I must go by tonight's train."

Anandibai immediately rushed into the kitchen and served dinner for her husband. Then she put a few things in a bag, while Mr Vasudevrav looked to see if he had sufficient money, and snatching the bag, he jumped into the carriage which had been ordered to return, and drove to the Victoria Station. On his way he stopped at a house where his head clerk resided, and told him to look after the affairs and the home people, and if there were any clients to send them to Mr Chitnis, a friend and neighbour of Mr Vasudevrav. He caught the train, and taking a first-class ticket seated himself wearily, expecting the worst of news.

Kaku and Anandibai did not dine, but sat up with heavy hearts.

No one had noticed Ratan except the maid, who washed her eyes, and then both walked right upstairs to the top room, and as Ratan lay down, the maid sang softly some Hindu airs which sent her to sleep. Ratan's father had come and gone, and she had been perfectly ignorant of this, and even of the arrival of the telegram. She was, however, made to rise just before the household retired and take a little supper, after which she went to bed. Anandibai lay awake by her daughter's side until early morning, when she managed to get sleep for about an hour. Kakubai was simply prostrate. Every now and then she would exclaim: "O Narayan! What will happen to Dinnanath? Oh! do not make his wife a widow I beseech of Thee, O God." She would, however, resign herself by saying, "We must submit to Fate."

It was a sad night, indeed; but all rose early and went about the daily duties. Mr Vasudevrav did not write or telegraph. He had gone, and with his return, he would bring the news, whether good or bad, and the poor, anxious people in the house waited for his return every day. On the fifth day, two carriages drove to the door in the early morning. Mr Vasudevrav got out of the first one; and, without saying a word, walked in, and flung himself on a sofa in a disturbed manner. Out of the second carriage a most astonishing and pitiful figure stepped out, and seated herself on the ground, weeping loudly. Then, bending her head, which was shaved but covered with her *padar*,[3] she knocked it against a huge stone, and became desperate with grief. Anandibai and Kakubai rushed to the door and beheld Dinnanath's widow. They shuddered at the sight. In the study they found Mr Vasudevrav prostrate but silent. The two ladies gave way to their feelings, but Vasudevrav, with emotion, told them to be quiet, and to take in the poor girl for his brother's sake. Then Kakubai wailed loudly, and said: "The wretch has swallowed our Dinu! Why did she marry him? To eat him up in this way! Why hast thou brought this ill luck into the house? She will surely swallow someone here. Our Dinu has gone, and she is nothing to us now," and the poor old lady shook and wailed most pitifully. The young widow again knocked her forehead against a stone in desperate grief. She would have indeed preferred to have followed her husband on the funeral pile. Her life was a blank now. The light—the god of her life—was no more. "What is the use of living!" thought she. She fell

---

[3] The end part of the sari.

backwards and appealed to the god of death. "Oh, Death! Carry me away," exclaimed the poor, stricken creature; and with the last word she fainted away. For two hours there was utter confusion, and no one would ask her to come in—not even the servant; and there she sat on the bare ground, crushed with grief, until she fainted away. The fainting and falling attracted the people of the house, and the servant was ordered to bring some water, which was sprinkled on her face; and when she came to herself, she was led into the verandah, where she sat down—a sight of pity and misery.

Poor little Ratan had now come to know of her uncle's illness and the cause of her father's journey. But all that had happened in the morning shocked her fearfully, for when the confusion and the weeping began, she simply stood aloof, and turned pale. She soon went to her mother's side; and, holding her *sari*, she gave way to convulsive sobs and cries, until the father took her near him and quieted her.

To turn now to the place where Mr Vasudevrav had proceeded after the arrival of the telegram.

The younger and only brother of Mr Vasudevrav was principal of a government high school at Nasik, and this year the great festival *Sinhasta* was going on. These pilgrimages and festivals are more or less the cause of the malady—cholera—in upcountry places, and as usual the cholera epidemic came, and carried off Mr Dinnanath, as well as a hundred others, leaving his wife, Tarabai, a widow of fourteen years.

Poor Tarabai had been married only the year before. Her father, Sittaram Krishnarav Sanzgiri, was a clerk in one of the government offices, and had died when Tara was but a child. Then her mother, Shantabai, who lived with a relative away in the Konkan, was too glad to get her little girl married to a man of position and learning, for she felt the burden of life immensely after the death of her husband. Six months after marriage it was thought that Tarabai was big enough to look after the household affairs, so when Dinnanath came to his brother for his holidays the last time, he took away his young bride to attend to the house, and if possible he meant to instruct her in the late hours of the evening. They lived very happily, but though it seemed a most fortunate lot for Tarabai, it was too soon embittered by the heavy blow she had now sustained in the death of her husband.

Mr Vasudevrav had been devoted to his brother, and his death was a great blow for him too. The poor girl widow could not be sent to her mother, for she lived in an out-of-the-way place, where people were very bigoted and foolish. So thinking the best thing would be to place his brother's wife under his shelter, he had brought her home.

The whole house now went into mourning, except Ratanbai, who no longer belonged to her own family, having been already married into another. The ladies were in the inner apartment, and friends, caste brothers and sisters, and relations came in hundreds to pay visits of condolence. Mr Vasudevrav kept to his office room, whither the gentlemen came. The ladies came and sat beside the mourners Anandibai and Kakubai. The young widow was in an inner apartment, prostrate on the ground. The mourners wept, and the visitors wept, and then the poor widow wailed loudly. Some of the old and ignorant ladies would even say hard things; but in all this visiting, no word of comfort or condolence was given to the stricken girl.

Ratanbai was very sad too, and she would nestle by her mother's side, and sob and weep. Anandibai and Kakubai could not touch anything for eleven days, so Ratan looked after the house, and made herself most useful and helpful. She had felt, however, very differently from her mother. Her young widowed aunt had touched her heart, and though she lamented the loss of her uncle immensely, yet she sorrowed more for the poor widow. She could not realize the change. Six months ago, when Tarabai had left the house to go to Nasik with *Kaka*,[4] how beautiful she was! Ratanbai had unfolded the new black sari which was given to her on the occasion of her aunt's departure to her new home. How sweet Tarabai looked in the lovely red cashmere shawl as she stepped into the landau, and drove to the station with her husband. "How nicely we got on; we got to

---

[4] Uncle.

be quite friends. I loved her," thought Ratanbai; and when she saw the same aunt, hardly to be recognized, *her* heart was not filled with hard and cruel thoughts. She loved her, and Ratan's resolution was to be kind to her while she kept house for the eleven days. She went to Tarabai every morning, and asked her to wash and take a little tea or milk. She again looked after her during midday, and saw that she slept comfortably at night. Many a time she sat by her, and said, "*Kaki*,[5] do not cry."

Whilst Ratanbai kept house, she rose earlier than usual, and first attended to the safe bringing in of the milk. They had two cows and a buffalo of their own. She took her bath, and next heated the milk on the fire, and poured it gently into brass cups, which she carried to the room of her mother and aunt. After asking her mother how much of the milk was to be kept for butter and curds, she accordingly gave orders to the servant in charge of these matters. Then she ordered breakfast; telling the cook what vegetables to prepare, and in what way they should be dressed. Her next occupation was to peel and cut up the potatoes carefully, and to wash the leafy vegetables. Then she went to the storeroom, which was near the kitchen, and gave out the provisions to the cook. At about that time, too, the cow-boy and the buffalo-man and the coachman came for their supplies, and Ratan stood with keys in hand, while they took out the necessary quantities. If money was needed by the servants for *bazar* purchases, she went to her mother, who threw to Ratan her purse,[6] telling her how much money to take out. Ratan, having thrown the purse again to her mother, would give the amount to the servants. Shortly before breakfast, Ratan undertook the duty of making bread (*polli* or *chupatties*), which her mother usually made, for Mr Vasudevrav always liked what his wife had cooked. Ratan therefore (in her *sovle*[7]) seated herself near the fireplace, with the kneaded flour and fresh *tup*[8] by her

[5] Dear Aunt.

[6] Her mother was a mourner, and as such might not come into contact with anyone.

[7] A silk sari.

[8] Clarified butter.

side and a board and rolling pin in front, to make the breakfast cakes. Adding plenty of butter, she rolled the dough again and again, clapping it between her tiny hands, it was then thrown into clean iron pan over a slow fire. Ratan meanwhile made another cake, still keeping an eye on the cake that was being cooked, which needed to be turned every minute. When she had made enough, she buttered and folded the cakes, placing them carefully in a vessel kept for them only. Washing her hands, she told the cook that the lowest three cakes were for her father and the next two for Kakubai. These two had always food that was specially prepared for them. The meals now had to be served in each one's apartment, and Ratan helped in all this. She saw that everyone had a nice clean plate and sufficient water. First she attended to her father, and then to her mother and to her aunts. She herself had her meals last of all, afterwards. Ratan then sat near a window on a low stool, with a quantity of rice near her, which she cleaned grain by grain to make it ready for cooking.[9] At about half past one, visitors arrived and went on coming, and Ratan then quietly sat by her mother. In the evening there was another plain meal, except that for Mr Vasudevrav something special was prepared, and Ratan always attended to this. Thus her days passed.

The days of the mourning were now over, and all went on as usual. Mr Vasudevrav, as a sign of mourning, put a white head dress on instead of a coloured one. The ladies dressed as usual. The shock of grief, however, did not leave the family for some time, and what had passed was in constant remembrance because of the young widow being in the house.

Ratanbai, after an absence of nearly a month, began again to go to school. The news of her uncle's death had already been made known to all, and amongst the friends who had visited the afflicted family, some had come from the school. For two months there were no further interruptions.

---

[9] This is a daily household occupation for the women.

Shevantibai Nikambe 31

A *Konkanastha* Brahmin family
(Copyright The British Library)

CHAPTER III

One evening Ratanbai on returning from school, rushed into the house, and embracing her mother, said: "Mother, dear, Mrs B——, who visits our school, has invited us to a party at her bungalow next week; and the teacher told us today all those who come regularly to school, and do the lessons well, will be taken to this party, so you will let me go every day, won't you?" pleaded the child. The mother promised; but Kakubai, who was near, said: "Why do you want to go to the English people's houses? They will give you something to eat, and defile you." And, turning to Ratan's mother, she added: "Anandi, you had better tell Ratan that she must not eat anything there."

Ratanbai: Is there any harm in eating the fruits?

Kakubai: No, you may have fruit, but do not touch anything else.

The day of the party arrived, and Ratan, who was regular at school came home early to dress. Her mother arranged her hair, and dressed her in a quiet but costly *sari*, allowing her no extra jewels except a nose ring. The girls were to start exactly at a quarter to four from the school, and Ratan was in the midst of the excited and happy party just ten minutes earlier. The carriages came one by one to the door, and the girls, in groups of five and six, took their seats, and drove up to Malabar Hill, to one of those beautiful bungalows which command a splendid view of the city and its surroundings. It was nearly eight o'clock when Ratanbai returned home, and after she had hurriedly thrown her shawl on the *chowphala*,[1] she sat down before Kakubai and began relating the evening's history. As Ratan began, Tarabai, who was in the inner apartment, drew closer to the door, and listened intently to her bright happy niece: "There were twelve carriages, and in each about six or seven sat. When we came to the house, Mrs B— and her daughter received us, and first we were taken into the cloakroom, where our shawls were kept, and each of us had a *veni* given her, which we put in our hair. Then we went upstairs into the *Diwankhana*. It was so pretty with mirrors and curtains, and pictures and piano. There were silk and satin sofas and chairs, and photographs were kept in silver frames. After a while we were told 'tea was ready'. At this the girls simply rose to their feet and said: 'No tea for us.' But Muktabai came near, and assured us that we were to have fruit and not tea. Then we went downstairs into the dining room. It is a large, beautiful room, with pretty pictures and mirrors, and any amount of glass things. There was a large table in the middle, and on it was a beautiful white cloth, and on this the plates, knives, forks, and glasses were arranged. There were fruits— mangoes, figs, grapes, oranges, plantains, custard apples, pineapples, and *pumbalows*. Beside these were *pedhe* and *barphi*.[2] All round this large table were chairs, and when we were told to take our seats it was such fun! We had never in our lives sat at table before, and at first we were all backward to do it; and when we did sit some of us made mistakes. Kamallabai and Nanibai sat together first on one chair, and we did laugh; Gangabai, while cutting a mango, cut her finger, and Balajipant, the Brahmin, had to take her outside to tie it up. Some girls sucked the mango instead of cutting it, and the juice all ran down over the clean white cloth; and one of the girls, while helping herself to an orange, hit a glass, which fell into bits on the floor."

Kakubai: Then you caused much damage to the poor, kind madam?

[1] Swing.
[2] Native sweets.

Ratanbai: But she was most kind. First, we told her that we could not sit at the table and eat, but she would not listen, and so we did our best. There were so many kinds of fruits, and the table looked so pretty with the flowers; and Balajipant was there to serve, so it was a regular Hindu repast.

Kakubai: After eating, how did you manage about the water?

Ratanbai: Oh, then we were taken outside to the pipe, and Balajipant gave us water, and then we went into the playground at the back and had games. We played one or two English games, but the girls enjoyed *zhima*[3] and *phugadi*[4] most. After a little rest we went again into the *Diwankhana*, and heard singing and playing. Mrs B—played the piano, and Miss B—sang. When Miss B—began I thought she was crying, but we were told afterwards that that was the way English ladies sing. After the singing, Mrs B—taught us a new game called "Thimble", and then I was asked to recite "Meddlesome Matty", and Dwarkabai and Manjulabai played a duet on the piano. When it got dark we were anxious to return home, and as we rose to go, Mrs B— came near and told us that we must go and spend such evenings with her often, for it had given her much pleasure to have us there. She told us to be good girls and attend school regularly, and before long there will be another party for us. Sonabai then carried in the tray of flowers which we had brought from school, and I put the garlands round their necks. They were glad—but so surprised! Then one of the elder girls came forward and said a few simple sentences in English to thank the ladies. After this we sang the Queen's *stotra*[5] and came downstairs. Mrs B—shook hands with us upstairs, and when we got into our carriages she came down and saw us again. She is so kind and beautiful, and

---

[3] *Zhima* is a game constantly played by girls. Four stand in a group, and they move on backwards and forwards in a circle, clasping one another's hands, and making a sharp noise with their finger and thumb. When the game is played fast, with many groups, it looks very graceful.

[4] *Phugadi* is played by two girls who stand opposite, their feet touching one another. They cross hands, and holding tightly, balance backwards and whirl round.

[5] Hymn.

her house is simply a little palace. The punkahs, the carpets, the curtains, and the mirrors were so pretty.

Here Ratan's mother said: "That will do now; have some supper, and talk about your party afterwards. The whole night will not suffice for you to tell about it all."

"I have had so many fruits and sweets today," said Ratanbai, "that I do not feel much inclined to have supper. But I will try a little rice and *sambare*."[6]

As Ratan rose to go, Kakubai, with a disturbed look on her face, began, "I cannot think what enjoyment the girls find in going to parties. Why do we want all this? It is not so very essential. Did we have these enjoyments in our days? And yet we grew up and prospered. Where did we go to school? Did we even handle a book? We went to the temples daily and worshipped *Maravti*. We did household work, and attended to *veni phani*.[7] The girls of these days want to go to school, to parties, to *sabhas*, and eat fruits from the *mlench*[8] hands. It is true the Brahmin served, but it was in the house of English people. We are Arya, but our Aryanism is getting all defiled. People are mad after English. Who are these English? Are not they incarnations of monkeys? Only the tail is not allowed them. What if they are rulers? We must not forget our caste and religion! Truly sin is raging, and the world is coming to an end. Oh Narayan! do thou open the eyes of the people!" Thus talked Kakubai; and giving a deep sigh, she stretched herself on the floor for a nap.

Ratan went to sleep rather excited and tired that evening.

For six weeks all went on as usual. Then came the *Shravana* month. It occurs about in August, and every young Hindu wife is then kept very busy.

The first day of the month fell on a Saturday. Everyone in Mr Vasudevrav's house was up at an early hour. Washing and bathing were finished before daybreak, and then hundreds of

---

[6] A very tasty dish made of the juice of lentils.
[7] The toilet.
[8] Unclean.

voices in the street were heard calling *shanvar vadha*.[9] The lowest caste women, with baskets on their heads, in which is an oil-can or bottle, a tin pot, etc., go on this day from door to door from a very early hour calling out *shanvar vadha*. Anandibai came out and beckoned one of the women, who, laying her basket on the floor, took out a half coconut shell and held it before Anandibai, who stood aloof, catching her *sari* carefully, so as not to touch the woman. Holding a small cup, full of sweet oil, Anandibai waved it over the unfortunate woman's head and poured it into the shell, and afterwards looked at her reflection in it. Then giving her a few small articles, Anandibai went indoors, and the woman, placing the oil in the basket, which she put on her head, went away shouting the same words. The waving of the oil and the giving it away meant that all the abuse, the misery, and unhappiness of the family would rest on this woman, and she was contented with her lot, for according to the *Shastras*, her caste is bound to take the curse and misery in that fashion, so that the gods may be pacified. Many a time, however, she does not find that misery follows, and she always likes to get a good quantity of the oil, which is real gain to her.

After a while Ratanbai came out with *her* cup of oil, and, beckoning one of the women, performed the same ceremony. The woman, instead of going away immediately, stood still and said, "*Bai saheb*, give me a *choli*; see, mine is all torn," showing a worn-out bodice on her body. Ratan ran in, and said to her mother, "Mother, dear, may I give my green silk *choli* to her? I do not wear it now, since the mango juice fell on it." To this her mother consented, and Ratan ran upstairs and fetched it, and held her hand forward for the woman to take it, but her mother saw her, and shouted, "Ratan, throw it at her, or else you will touch her." So Ratan, rolling it into a ball, threw it into the basket. The woman's eyes glistened, and her face beamed as she took it into her hand and looked at it, and with blessings and thanks, intimating that she would surely come the next Saturday, went away. The rest of the day was spent as usual.

[9] Please give alms on Shravana Saturday!

The *Shravana* Monday is always observed as a fast, and there are four of these fasts. Ratan rose as usual, and took a little milk before going to school. This was allowed her, because of her delicate constitution. Her mother and others fasted the whole day. The schools for girls at this season are always closed at one o'clock on Mondays, for the married girls and others arrive at school fasting. At one, then, Ratan returned home, and she was hungry, so was allowed to take fruits. Fasting means generally going without *cooked* food; milk, fruits, and sweets are allowed. In the evening they all bathed, and broke their fast by taking a simple meal.

The *Shravana mangalwar,* commonly known among the Hindu ladies as the *mangalagavri* day, is a great day with the newly married girls. Ratan had been married now for more than a year, so she had nothing to do regarding it in her own home; but she was invited by a sister-in-law, who was newly married, and who thus had to keep the festival. On *mangalagavri* Tuesday Ratan, therefore, did not go to school, for she had to be at her father-in-law's, and she was to return home to go to Walkeshwar to attend the *puja* of the goddess at her sister-in-law's house. At two o'clock she dressed, and, with her mother, drove to Malabar Hill. Both the mother and daughter were received most warmly, and were led into a large room, where a number of young wives, dressed very charmingly in their best *saris,* were seated on the floor most comfortably, talking in a noisy fashion. Among the young wives were some of Ratan's school companions. In a couple of minutes Ratan was in the midst of her friends, enjoying herself thoroughly. The mothers sat in groups also apart, and there was such a great noise, as all were talking, young and old—not, however, about the goddess, they were gossiping as to matters pertaining to themselves. The young people talked about school and home and *sasar.* In the meantime, Hirabai, Ratan's sister-in-law, fetched a matchbox, and, walking towards the side where the shrine was adorned with lamps, candles, flowers, and a thousand ornaments, lighted the lamps. Anandibai, who was carefully examining the arrangements, said, "*Mangalagavri* is too far back, place her a little forward, Hiroo."

The young girl, who was dressed very prettily in yellow silk with silver trimming, lifted the folds of her *sari* in front, and stretching her small but jewelled arm, brought the goddess a little forward, and then turned to ask if it would do. "Yes," said Anandibai; and the little wife went on with her business of worshipping it in the customary manner. Then, after treating her young friends with sweets, etc., the ceremony was at an end. Before seven o'clock all the guests went away, and so did Ratan and her mother. This ceremony had to be performed the following three Tuesdays, and Ratanbai was always invited, so she and her friends had some pleasant meetings.

The *shravana* month, however, came to an end, and Ratanbai rejoiced to be once more regular at her studies. For a month she was able to go to school.

One afternoon, a distant relative called on Anandibai, and in the course of her conversation said: "I was at your Ratanbai's mother-in-law's, and your *Vihinbai*[10] said, 'When Ratanbai is with us we never send her to school; but her parents are inclined to be of the "reformed" party; and she, being the only child, they pet her, and send her just because *she* likes to go; but they should consider our wish in the matter, and not allow her to attend school.'"

Both Kakubai and Anandibai were very troubled to hear this remark, and Kakubai, said, "Anandi, tell Vasudev this tonight and do not allow Ratan to go to school from tomorrow." Anandibai was very sorry for Ratan's sake, for though she herself was opposed to educating her daughter, she allowed matters to take their course, because dear Ratan was so fond of her school and teachers.

Ratan, as usual, returned home in the evening, and after having washed and taken her "meal", she began to help her mother in the small household duties. Anandibai was a sensible lady, and knowing how it would hurt her child to hear what her mother-in-law had been saying to people all over the town, she kept silent. In the evening, when Mr Vasudevrav returned

[10] The term used by the mother for the child's mother-in-law.

home, the thing was secretly unfolded to him by his wife. But he took no notice of it. Then later on Anandibai again spoke to him about it, and he simply said, "Do as you please, Anandi. I do not know when you women will understand matters rightly." Here Kakubai interrupted. "Oh, Vasudev, you must remove the girl from school. If her *sasar's* people do not wish it, why should we go against them? You must save her from the *zach*[11] she will have." The old lady managed to persuade him, and at last it was decided that Ratan should not go to school from the next day.

Mr Vasudevrav was very, very sorry; but because they would not treat the question with reasonable consideration, he got tired of their arguments, and said, rather hastily, "Very well, remove her."

Ratanbai was kept in perfect ignorance of all this, and her mother was thinking as to how to tell her that she was not to go to school any more. Anandibai's anxieties were, for the present, soon over, for early the next morning a coconut arrived from Anandibai's sister Champubai's house, and that meant that a son was born. This was, indeed, happy news to all, and like an answer to her anxious prayer, for now the mother could prevent Ratanbai for a day, at least, on account of this news. The poor child was near her at the time the coconut arrived, and Anandibai, after having joyfully replied to the bearer that she would be there after the meal, gently said to her girl, "Ratanbai, we will go to *mavashi*,[12] so do not go to school, dear, today." To this the child assented, though in a disappointed manner.

After breakfast, Anandibai hurried to her sister's with her daughter to see the newborn babe. They spent a few hours in Champubai's room. Anandibai sat and stood at a distance while she, with Ratan, looked at her new nephew. The little fellow was stared at very minutely, and after careful examination it was pronounced that he promised to be fair like the mother—to the satisfaction of all.

[11] Ill treatment.
[12] Aunt.

Amongst the many lady visitors (who were mostly relatives) Anandibai's elder sister was there. She informed all of her intended visit to Goa. The day for starting, she said, was fixed for the following Monday.

As Ratan had gone into another room with the young companions who, like herself, had come with their mothers, Anandibai said to her sister, "Will you take our Ratanbai to Goa, too? I must, however, ask her mother-in-law. We have now removed her from school, and I want her to be occupied, as she will, I fear, take it to heart; and besides, it will be a nice change for her to go with you and Kamalla. Take her to the temples there and show her our gods."

"If her mother-in-law allows her I shall take her; she will be good company to our Kamalla," said the sister, whose name was Sonabai. It was then decided to ask Ratanbai's mother-in-law, and if she consented to send her with Sonabai, her elder *mavashi*. After partaking of refreshments, Anandibai rose to depart. Catching the corner of her *padar*, and bringing it under her armpit round her waist, where she tucked it, and throwing her handsome grey cashmere shawl across her shoulders, she took leave of her very revered mother, promising at the same time to come every day to see Champu.

The first thing Anandibai did after she got home was to send a most respectful message over to Ratan's mother-in-law asking her opinion about Ratan's accompanying her aunt Sonabai to Goa. To this the reply came, "Send her anywhere, but do not send her to school." It was, then, thus settled, but Ratanbai was kept in ignorance of her being removed from school. She was told to go to school and take two months' leave, to pay the fees for those months, and to tell the *Bai* that she was going to Goa with her aunt. Ratan obeyed sadly and reluctantly, and the teachers and the girls were very sorry indeed to lose her, though they were led to suppose, for a time only. Now, Mr Vasudevrav's consent was to be obtained, and that duty was left to strict old Kakubai, who after an unpleasant struggle of four days, succeeded; and the next day Ratanbai with a heavy heart started for Goa. The party consisted of eleven, including the servants. Ratan felt sad leaving her parents, as they did, too, at parting from her; but she was very soon happy again, as she was with aunt Sonabai and her cousin Kamalla, to whom she was devoted. Before her marriage she used to spend a great deal of her time at her aunt's, and now, too, every now and then a special invitation was often sent to her to spend the day or evening with them. Anandibai and Kakubai, who could not help their tears when saying goodbye, were aware that she would be at ease with Sonabai and her children.

The party for Goa started early in the morning from the Carnac Bunder, in one of the coasting steamers, for Vengurle, where they landed by sunset. Relatives who had been written to beforehand were on the pier to receive them. Soon they find themselves in one of the old-fashioned but strongly built houses in the heart of the town. They did not do much talking, as the seasickness, which had attacked almost all of them, made them quiet. A good tempting meal had been prepared for them, but though they sat *at the leaves*,[13] they only attempted to eat a few mouthfuls. This country home, though owned by a very wealthy family, was furnished according to old customs of the place. There were no chairs, bedsteads, or tables. The ground served instead for everything. There was an upper storey, and, in a large airy room, mattresses were most comfortably laid, where the beds had been arranged by the servants. The young people all retired just as they were. Sonabai and the ladies sat up talking for a while before retiring. The mother, with her four children and Ratan, all slept in a row. On the other side lay two other ladies with their five children. A dim light was kept burning the whole night.

Ratan was the first one to awake in the morning. She had had a good rest, and felt refreshed. She half lifted hereself, and looking round, saw that all were asleep. Laying her untidy head on the low pillow, she gazed out of the open window at the lovely clear sky, and her thoughts wandered to her home and her mother. Then gently touching her cousin Kamalla, who lay

---

[13] Portions of plantain leaves are still often used instead of plates.

rolled up in a sheet, she said, "Kamalla, get up." Her cousin, without saying a word or even opening her eyes, covered herself in the sheet, and turned her back to Ratan. So Ratan turned to the other side, and found her little boy cousin smiling gleefully, and kicking his fat little limbs. She played with him until something displeased him, and then he set up a terrible shriek, which woke all in the room. The servants were up, and were now busy getting the baths ready. By eleven o'clock the whole household was up. Bathing over, they sat down to a substantial breakfast. The rice, bread, milk, and butter all tasted most delicious. After breakfast, a little loitering about took place, and arrangements were made for the onward journey. In the afternoon, some of the shrines in the town were visited, and though Ratan was feeling very strange, yet she enjoyed it all.

The following day they started for the next place, and two months were spent in visiting the temples and shrines and in travelling. During this time Ratanbai constantly wrote to her teachers and school friends of the pleasant time she was having. Here is one of her letters:—

Sawantwadi, Nov. 13.

My dear Manjulabai,—Much affectionate respect. I received your letter, and I was very glad to read the news. Now our next address is *Ganpat Shanturam Vaidya's* house, No. 2, Kolapur. We visited the shrine of—and worshipped them. We bathed in the tank, too. We went to the *Vada*[14] and saw the *Rani Saheb*.

The hills and the valleys are beautiful, and the air so pleasant. We do not know when we shall return. I am, however, enjoying the travelling. Remember me most gratefully to all the teachers.

When we went to see the *Rani Saheb*, she made me sing, and asked me many things. I am so sorry to lose my lessons, but you must let me know the lessons you are learning, and as I have brought a few books with me, I will learn them up, so as not to fall too behind. I hope all at home are quite well.—Your dear friend,

Ratan

[14] Palace.

The teachers, knowing Ratanbai was out of town, were not surprised at her absence; but one morning, one of the girls brought the news to school that she was never coming again. This news was received with much disappointment. Ratanbai and her aunt stayed away for a fortnight longer than had been intended, and after their return Ratan was sent to her mother-in-law's; it was there only that she came to know she was not to go to school any more. Never was she to handle a book now. "I wish I had known how to converse in English. *Sasubai* should have kept me at school till then; no pleasure or interest for me now. Oh! what shall I do with myself the whole day?" The young girl's heart was full of grief; but she knew she must submit to the *Sasu's* rule, and she tried to be brave about it.

Four months passed, and Ratan's life grew dull and cheerless. She did not know how to while away the time without books or some sort of pleasant occupation. She did attend to the household duties: sometimes she sat cleaning the rice, sometimes sewing, or she had to make the sweets; but, literally, her day was mostly spent in doing nothing. At the mother-in-law's, she would simply sit through the long hours of the day with her mother-in-law and the other ignorant lady, and they would stare out of the windows from time to time or fall asleep on the mat. Ratanbai was most miserable, and she longed to be at school. How often, with an aching heart, she would sit dreaming about the school life! Her teacher, her companions, her singing lesson, the English lesson, the translation class, came before her, and then the longing would come: "Oh! could I but go to school once again!"

A group of high-caste young Hindu wives
In Mrs Nikambe's school
(Copyright The British Library)

CHAPTER IV

Though Ratan was taken from school, she was allowed, whenever she was at her father's, to pay a visit to her friends at the school house. Her young husband, Prataprao, was permitted to continue his studies, in spite of the threatening difficulties since his father's death. A distant relative was meantime appointed to look after his father's estate. Prataprao attended the Wilson College, and here the sound education he received, and the exemplary lives he came in contact with day after day, made a great impression on his young heart, and prepared him for the life before him. In appearance he was inclined to be tall and slender. His complexion was fair, his eyes were dark and bright. He dressed, like all Hindu students, in a *dhotar*[1] and long coat. His head was always covered with the prettiest of embroidered caps. He wore his *bikbali,* and gold ring, and his dear father's gold watch and chain. He was very fond of his mother, and respected her much. His two sisters and a younger brother loved their *dada,*[2] and looked up to him as a pillar in the family now, since their father's death.

When Ratan was removed from school, Prataprao was in his BA course. Six months passed; Nagnathrav, the husband of Ratanbai's cousin, Kamallabai, was successful in the BA examination of the Bombay University, and won a medal. So

[1] The Hindu gentleman's dress.
[2] Elder brother.

rejoiced were his parents at this event that they told their son he might ask for any present, however costly, and they would give it him in memory of this brilliant success. The young man, instead of asking for a diamond ring, or a horse and carriage, said to his father, "Father, nothing will give me so much pleasure as to see my wife being educated at a good school. If my choice is asked, may I request you to prevail upon mother to consent to this only?" The request was made known to the loving mother, who, though disappointed, granted it for her darling boy's sake; thus they all began thinking about sending Kamallabai to school. Within a week's time it was settled, and as Kamalla would be very lonely at school, it was suggested that Mr Vasudevrav be asked to allow Ratanbai to accompany her for a few months.

When, however, Mr Rambhao (Kamalla's father-in-law) came to Mr Vasudevrav, the latter said, "I am sorry to say my daughter is not in my hands. If you can persuade her mother-in-law and the other lady, Kashinathpant's wife, in the matter, nothing will give me more pleasure, for I am in favour of our girls and women being educated. If some lady were to open a class for the married ladies, I would be the first one to send Anandi. I am thinking, however, of getting a native lady to come to my house and teach her. If Ratan were in my charge, I would send her to school today. I would not have allowed her to be kept at home at this early age, when she was getting on nicely, too; but our girls are not ours when married!"

Mr Rambhao was well acquainted with Ratan's father-in-law's people, so one evening he went to them for a friendly visit. After a long talk on various matters, the subject was introduced, and so heartily was it taken up by Mr Kashinathpant (Ratan's late father-in-law's brother) that he at once went towards the apartment of his widowed sister-in-law, and, standing by the half-open door, said: "Rambhao has come. He is going to send his daughter-in-law to school. Her husband, Nagnath, has passed the BA examination, and has gained a big prize. Which school shall we recommend for Kamalla? Do you know anything of Ratanbai's school?"

Ratan's mother-in-law came near the door, but without showing herself—the door being half closed—and said: "Yes, it is a nice school, and the only one where big girls go."

"Do you know who ought to be seen there?"

"No; but Ratan would know."

Here Mr Rambhao rose, and coming near the door, said: "Our Kamalla is very shy, and would like to have a companion until she gets used to the school; so will you have any objection to send Ratanbai with her?"

Ratanbai's mother-in-law did not answer for a while. Then she said, "I will ask my *Bala*"[3] (Ratan's husband, Prataprao).

Mr Rambhao knew *Bala* well; so now his next duty was to catch hold of him immediately. After spending the evening very happily, he rose and took leave, and was walking out of the compound, when, to his surprise and pleasure, Prataprao, who was returning home from a Sunday evening lecture in the college, stood before him. After exchanging greetings, Mr Rambhao and he walked out together, and went to the sea beach. It was a lovely moonlit night; the clouds had all rolled away, and the stars were dimly twinkling overhead. The Back Bay waters lay cool and smooth in the basin, and just where Mr Rambhao with Ratan's husband stood, the playful waves ran in and out between the black stones. The city was chiefly lit up by this lovely silvery atmosphere, though a few dim lights could be seen. They stood on the beach admiring nature in her evening attire. Behind them were the new-fashioned dwelling houses recently erected and half occupied. They walked up and down the paved path, and then down to the sands, and seated themselves on a large piece of rock. Mr Rambhao talked on many matters, and then began about education, just to see Prataprao's turn of mind about it, and to his great happiness he found that Ratan's husband was in favour of education for women. Mr Rambhao then spoke to him about the young wives being educated, told him of the attempt they were making to send Kamallabai to school, and at last asked Prataprao to consent

---

[3] A pet name.

to Ratan's going, should his mother speak to him about it. Prataprao quietly listened, and assented to the final request. Within an hour each went to his house. Mr Rambhao had gained his object, and it is no exaggeration to say that young Prataprao was happy.

After two weeks, on a bright Tuesday morning, Ratan was dressed in a pretty navy blue *sari* (a favourite among her *saris*), with a handsome silk border. It was worked in Indian embroidery, with white cotton. She looked charming with her bright red Brahmin shoes, and the gracefully folded dress and the flower wreath in her hair. A new bag was in her hand, and she carefully put in it her old books and other school necessaries. "Mother, dear, I feel ashamed to go to school now," Ratan said. "Won't the girls laugh at me?" "Why will the girls laugh?" replied Anandibai. "You know them all, and you like going to school. Besides, Kamalla will be constantly with you." Just then the carriage came to the door, a victoria with a beautiful brown horse. Ratanbai put on her *shalu* while the *Bhaya* placed her bag in the carriage. She lightly stepped in, the *Bhaya* attending on her. Driving to Kamalla's house, and taking her up, they went on towards the school. The teachers and the girls were delighted to see Ratanbai among them again, and they welcomed her cousin most cordially. The time passed very happily. As the singing teacher did not come, the girls were allowed a longer recess, and Ratan joined in all the games. So did Kamalla, who was already pleased with the school and her companions, and thought the life there was indeed happy and bright. In the afternoon, when the lessons were being taken, Ratan found herself very behind her classmates. When she was told to sit in the lower standard she did not like it, and said to her teacher, "Instead of going into the lower standard, may I go on with the class? I will ask father to find a teacher for me at home, and with him I will work up the back lessons." She said this in such a resolute but sweet way that the teacher gave her a fortnight's trial; within that period, if she did not show progress, it would be clear that she must stay in the lower class. Her cousin Kamalla was put in the "extra" class, where the new girls were prepared in the necessary subjects. Ratan assented to her teacher's arrangement by saying, "I will learn all the lessons." She and her cousin left at the usual hour, and each had much to tell to the ladies at home. It was arranged by Mr Vasudevrav that the victoria should be at the disposal of Ratan for her school, and that she should always call for Kamalla on the way, and drop her on the way back.

Ratan was now very happy with her studies. At home she had a teacher morning and evening, and in school all her spare moments were either spent with a book in hand or at her desk writing some exercise. The fortnight passed, and the day for Ratanbai's examination arrived. It took three hours. All her exercise books she showed first; every lesson up to date was neatly written. Then she read, spelt, translated, did some writing and arithmetic, grammar, history, and geography, and in all except geography she did well. The manner in which she had taken pains and persevered, pleased the teacher greatly, and she was told to sit in her class with the old companions. Ratan was delighted, and she resolved now to take more pains with her lessons.

Ratan's mother-in-law consented to her going to school at the desire of Prataprao. She was allowed to continue for some months, and she tried to make the best of the opportunity allowed her.

After six months, however, discouragement came. Ratanbai's husband failed in his BA examination, which was a great disappointment to all. But Ratan, about the same time, passed in the annual examination of the school very successfully, and was to receive the first prize in the class at the prize distribution to be held in about a month's time. These two incidents—her husband having failed, and she having passed in her school examination—were thought of very seriously by the ladies of Ratan's *sasar*, and the result was that her mother-in-law sent word to Mr Vasudevrav that her daughter-in-law should be immediately taken from school.

The message came through a relative, and was delivered in the presence of Ratanbai. As soon as she heard it, she flung herself on her mother's neck, and wept. "*Baba*,"[4] she said, "do let me go till the prize-giving! I am to get a prize, and the Governor's lady is coming. Oh, do let me stay till then!" The relative, who was an elderly old-fashioned lady, said to Ratan, "Your husband has failed, and what do you want with school and prizes now? Pray to the gods, go to the temples and pay the vows, that *he* may have success."

Ratan kept silent. She did feel so sorry, and the disappointment could be seen in her sad face. That evening she went upstairs to the top room and cried herself to sleep. She refused to rise and have supper, and when her mother went to her she simply wept.

After much discussion that night between the ladies and Mr Vasudevrav, it was decided that Ratan should not attend school any more, and that she must stay away from the very next day. It greatly disheartened her, and Mr Vasudevrav was sorry for Ratan's sake, but more so on account of her husband. Her cousin Kamallabai felt very grieved, and though she had got to like the school and the girls, she greatly missed Ratan.

The next day an invitation arrived for Ratan to go and stay a few weeks at Bandora, a suburb near Bombay, and on the following Saturday, Kamalla and Ratan, with two servants and a host of boy cousins, travelled thither. Ratan's grandmother lived here with her two married sons. A little cousin baby—the first and only child in this house—had died a fortnight ago, and as the house looked dull and gloomy, the children, with Ratan and Kamalla, were asked to spend a few days with the family, so that it might be made more cheerful. The little boys were found to be very troublesome and self-willed, and so were sent back to Bombay after four days—Ratan and Kamalla stayed longer. During this time, they not only helped to lighten the sad home, but had many a talk by themselves, which helped to increase their mutual attachment.

They took long walks and drives by the beach with their aunts, and had a time of real change and rest. After four weeks,

---

[4] Father.

Kamallabai was obliged to return for school to Bombay, so Ratan was left alone. Her aunts were very fond of her, and made much of her, and did not allow her to be lonely or sad. After two months, the grandmother, with her two daughters-in-law, came to Bombay, and Ratan accompanied them, and returned home.

Prataprao, in his disappointment, had not at first noticed how his girl-wife was treated, but when he set to his studies with a resolute will, he quietly spoke to his mother about Ratan being sent again to school. His request was very reluctantly granted. Kashinathpant's wife tried to interfere, but somehow the young husband was successful in this effort. By-and-by, as the days of his examination drew near, Ratan's mother-in-law thought that if her son should succeed, his wife might be kept longer at school in spite of the hateful remarks of the caste brethren.

The month of December arrived, with the examination, and Ratan was kept at home to make offerings to the gods that there might be success. A month after, when the results were declared, she came to school with a bright beaming face, saying nothing, however, but simply greeting everyone with a smiling countenance. All knew that her husband had passed his examination. During the "recess" hour one of the girls brought to her the *Times of India*, in which was the list of the successful candidates. Ratanbai quickly glanced down the list, and came to the name which, according to custom, never passed her lips except in a song or a rhyme. She burst out laughing to her heart's content, as half-a-dozen young wives repeated the name *Pratap Harischandra Khote* aloud. She again took the paper, and read aloud two or three names of the husbands of her friends who were among the successful candidates of some other examination. All who knew Prataprao congratulated him on his success, and especially his relatives, who were very happy, encouraged him to go to England. This event greatly encouraged Ratan, and she now resolved more than ever to take pains with her studies.

About eight months had passed, and the clever, persevering Ratanbai appeared to her teachers to be growing into a careless girl. Day after day, whenever she came to school from her mother-in-law's, she did not know her lessons, nor did she write any home exercises.

As she had been one of the best girls, for a couple of months she was forgiven and was not "kept in". At last matters came to such a pass that she could not be allowed to escape without being punished. One day she was made to sit in the "kept in" class, and was very ashamed, but she said to her friends, "It is better to learn here than not learn at all," and she without murmur quietly submitted to the punishment. Just before going home, Ratan went to see her teacher, who said to her, "I do not like to see you, Ratan, in the 'kept in' class. Won't you now take pains, and give no further trouble?" To this the little wife simply nodded.

About twelve days after, one morning Ratanbai walked into the school house with swollen eyes, biting her lips. She threw her shawl down in the room and rushed into the Girls' Room upstairs, and, throwing herself on the sofa, burst out crying, and sobbed and sobbed until her cousin came and sat by her.

Kamalla: What is the matter, Ratanbai?

Ratan (sobbing): Oh, dear. What shall I do?

Kamalla: But tell me what is the matter? Is anyone ill? Or did *Sasu* scold you?

Ratan had hid her face in her *padar*, and, wiping her eyes, she said—No, I can bear *Sasubai*'s scolding. I wish it was her scolding!

Kamalla: Then what is it—tell me, can't you?

Ratan: See, the door is open and someone will hear us. If the classes have gone into the rooms for lessons, go and ask the teacher if you may sit with me for a while, and then I will tell you. Here, Ratan's eyes filled with tears, and her face was covered in her *padar*.

Kamallabai went to ask for the permission, which was fortunately granted, and the door having been locked from the inside, Ratan began to pour her troubles.

Ratanbai: "She will not rest until she sees me away from school. Everything has been done to prejudice my mind about education, but I have held on, and, somehow, by God's help, things have fallen to my lot happily. All these days I have been scolded and punished in school for not learning my lessons properly, and I have had to bear another trouble at home; for I am never allowed to open my bag or to handle a book. Vithabai has made it her business of late to keep me away from school. In the evenings, when I go home, some work is sure to be ready for me, and I must attend to it. Then, when I *have* spare time, I must sit on the swing and gossip about all sorts of rubbish or listen to the novels, and before it is nine I must be in bed. My mornings are spent in nearly the same way, only we are busier, for the breakfast is required early. But there is not so much work after all. You know Vithabai and her nature; she is against education, and therefore is trying her best to remove me from school. I cannot speak to *Sasubai*, because sometimes she tells things to *Sasubai* in such a way that I get the worst of it, so I just keep quiet."

Kamalla: And we dare not tell at our *Mahera*[5] what happens at *Sasar*.
Ratan: Oh, no!
Kamalla: Tell me, what happened today.
Ratan: Oh, dear! All these days she tried her best to prejudice my mind, and now today it has gone so far that I do not know what to do. Here, Ratanbai buried her face in her *padar* and burst out crying, and went on sobbing and weeping for about a quarter of an hour. Kamallabai could not bear to see her cousin so unhappy, and she, too, sat with her *padar* to her eyes and told Ratan to be quiet. They composed themselves, and Ratanbai began: "This morning I went about as usual in the house. I served the breakfast, and helped in matters here and there. When it was ten I got ready for school. Bringing my shawl and bag out, I asked Vithabai if I might go. To this she said—" here Ratan's eyes again filled with tears, and her *padar* was up to her face again. After a pause she continued—"I was just asking, when she said, 'School! school! school! Wait, let Prataprao come this

---

[5] Father's house.

evening, I will tell him that I saw you looking at the gardener with an evil eye, and then after your mother-in-law comes to know of it we shall see how you will go to school,'" and Ratan, who was sitting erect, flung herself backward, and burying her face in her arms and *padar*, sobbed most bitterly, only saying now and then, "Oh, dear! what shall I do?" The two girls sat together, one shocked and the other giving way to convulsive sobs. No one else knew the secret of Ratan's persecution. Both girls went home that evening with hearts full of thought and anxiety.

The next few days Ratan did not go to school. One afternoon, as she sat before her mother-in-law with folded hands, a servant came from her father's house, and saluting, said, "Rao *Saheb* has sent me to fetch Ratanbai. *Bai Saheb* has been ill since last night." Ratan, hearing this, turned pale, and looked at her mother-in-law, waiting for the consent as to whether she might go. Her mother-in-law told her to go, and she flew into the room for her shawl, which she threw hurriedly over her shoulders, asking, "Where is the carriage?" She was told it was out on the road. With tears in her eyes she took leave of her mother-in-law, and rushed through the garden, and took her seat in the carriage. They drove very fast, and she was soon at the door. There was great confusion. Four doctors were in the house. The neighbouring ladies had come in. Mr Vasudevrav was wringing his hands, and Kakubai and the other ladies were weeping. Ratan did not know what to do. At last Kaku caught sight of her, and wailed loudly, "Ratan, dear Ratan, come and see *ayee*."[6] Ratan went, and oh! the sight she beheld. Her mother lay lifeless and pale on a bed. The crowd about her were in terror, and were waiting for the doctors' verdict. Ratan could not believe that was her mother. She looked about the room, and fainted away. The doctors attended to her and sent her to another apartment. After the usual examination, it was said that Anandibai had died of some affliction of the heart. The blow was terrible. The news soon spread throughout the town. The priests were informed

[6] Mother.

of it, and they came with the materials for the bier. Anandibai was immediately bathed and dressed in yellow. Her forehead was rubbed with the *kunku*; and flowers in garlands and loose were scattered over her body. Relatives and friends in hundreds flocked to Mr Vasudevrav's house. There was a good deal of wailing and crying; and as the body was being carried to be laid on the bier, it was heartrending to hear the continued weeping. Mr Vasudevrav groaned, and Ratan threw herself on the bier. The funeral dress of the men, whose heads were bare, was entirely white. A coconut was placed in Anandibai's hands, and four gentlemen lifted the bier, and away it went amidst the din and wailing of all the ladies and the gentlemen who stayed behind. Anandibai's remains were carried through the town in a procession, and the funeral was attended by six hundred gentlemen.

By ten o'clock all was finished.

The woman who so devotedly and faithfully filled her position as wife, mother, and sister was no more. The house looked desolate, and Mr Vasudevrav could not believe that he was still in this world. As for poor Ratan, who can describe the pain in that troubled young heart?

For eleven days friends and acquaintances crowded in after one o'clock to pay their visits of condolence. Mr Vasudevrav, as a sign of mourning, shaved off his moustache and dressed in white. Numbers came to comfort the family, and the relatives flocked round Mr Vasudevrav. On the seventh day, the bathing and purification took place. Still friends kept on coming for about a month. Ratan went to her aunt Sonabai, and Kakubai and Tarabai went to Bandora. Poor Tarabai was very unkindly treated, because of this unhappy event. Kakubai in her wailing often said, "Tara, you have brought this ill luck, and you have been the cause of our misery."

One day, at Bandora, Kakubai spoke very, very unkindly to the young widow, who thinking that she really was the cause of misery to others, resolved to do away with her life. She generally went to bathe on the beach, which was five minutes' walk from their house. After having planned all, she went out one morning early, and was in the act of throwing herself into the sea when a Hindu reformer, who was taking a walk, saw her and went to her rescue. He knew that the cause of this calamity was ill-treatment, as Tara's very appearance betrayed that she was a girl widow. This eventually led to her being sent to a Widows' Home with Mr Vasudevrav's consent.

Days passed very quietly now. At last the October vacation came. Mr Vasudevrav did not this time go, as usual, to his house in the country, but went away to the north, visiting the ancient and sacred places. Ratanbai continued to stay with her aunt until her father's return, spending the latter part of the time with her mother-in-law.

* * *

Five years have rolled away. Mr Vasudevrav looks much older; Ratan's husband has been to London, and has studied during three years for the Bar. At the time of his departure he left strict instructions, which were carried out, that Ratan should be sent to school until his return home. Tarabai is still in the Home, where she has studied and been trained as a teacher. She looks very sweet in her "reformed" dress. Her hair has grown again. Her head is no longer covered, but like the other ladies she wears her *padar* on the shoulder. She has no *kunku* and no ornaments, not even glass bangles. She wears a print jacket, and puts on a shawl when out of doors. Kakubai is shocked at the new ways in the family. She does not like the idea of Ratan going to school, nor does she approve of Tara's education, nor of Ratan's husband's going to England. She has asked Mr Vasudevrav for a considerable sum of money, which he has granted her, and she has set out on a long pilgrimage. There was a great blank in the family circle while Ratan's husband was in England.

After a successful career he has returned home, *via* America, Japan, and China, visiting the interesting places on the way.

About a week after his arrival, one beautiful day, the people at Ratanbai's *sasar* seemed to be unusually busy. There is a great bustle among the ladies, and preparations were being made for a quiet ceremony in the evening. The time arrives, and the guests, all ladies, drop in one by one. They are dressed very quietly. The little children are dressed in their pretty costumes. In the inner apartment two pretty seats with lighted lamps, and silver utensils, are facing each other. The ladies and the children all squat on the floor in front. By and by Prataprao walks in and takes his seat on one of the low stools. Then follows Ratanbai, who is dressed in the most charming ruby-coloured *pilao*, with jewels and flowers, looks a select *ratna*[7] herself. She bashfully and gracefully stands on the opposite stool, and drawing the silver utensils (basin and water jug) closer, says:—

> The water is clean and the silver is pure,
> May Prataprao's fame ever endure.

At this the young husband allows his wife to wash his feet in the silver basin. She soon dries them with a towel; then taking some scented powder says:—

> Spring has come and birds do sing,
> But Prataprao's virtues joy will bring.

To his arms then this powder is applied. Then she draws a large tray, and holding a huge garland of flowers says:—

> Flowers and foliage are pretty to behold.
> Prataprao's name gives delight untold.

when the garland is put round her husband's neck.

Then she gives the bouquet in his hand, and while doing so says:—

> Great were the men who adorned our land;
> And greater be Prataprao of the band.

[7] Jewel.

The *panvida*[8] is then given, and when doing so she says again:—

Spring is the best season of all;
May richest blessings on Prataprao fall.

Ratan's rhymes were listened to very attentively by the ladies. She soon took her seat on the stool, when Prataprao took up a flower wreath in his hand, and said:—

It rains, it lightens, it thunders!
Ratan, mind don't you make any blunders.

and gives the wreath in Ratan's hand, who then and there puts it into her hair.

While giving the scent he said:—

In this house you are installed as queen;
Therefore, Ratan, let your good example by all be seen.

Then the *vida* is given, and Prataprao says while giving:—

Ratan has prayed for blessings on me;
I in return, dear, pray the same for thee.

The husband and wife, without exchanging any words or looks, rise quietly; Ratan mixes amongst the ladies, and Prataprao goes silently into the drawing room. The dinner immediately follows, and whenever it is Ratanbai's turn to serve some joke is passed round among the children, who do their best to keep Prataprao lively.

The guests go away after the dinner, and in the newly furnished room upstairs Ratanbai is looking at the numerous presents on the table and writing desk when her eye falls on a beautifully bound gilt-edged Book. She grasps it, and is about to open it, when Prataprao, who is by her, seeing his young wife

---

[8] The folded leaf.

admiring the Book says: "I must have this Book on my table every day; there are a great many nice things in it which you must know." To this Ratanbai said: "I have this Book too." "Well," said her husband as he looked into his young partner's face, "then let yours be out too, and we shall make it our guide in life."

Thus Prataprao Khote claims young Ratanbai as his partner in life. They begin life together, recognizing the responsibilities and duties which lie before them, and which concern not only themselves but their people and their country.

Shevantibai M. Nikambe

J.S. Phillips 121 Fleet Street, London, E.C.

DIACRITICS USED IN THE FIRST EDITION

All diacritics that were used within the text in the first edition (together with the omitted few) are listed below.

Anandibai	Ānandībai
ayer	āī
baba	bābā
bai	bāi
bala	bālā
Balajipant	Bālājīpant
barphi	barphī
Bhatin	Bhātin
Bhaya	Bhāyā
bikbali	bikbalī
Brahmin	Brāhmin
Champubai	Champubāi
choli	cholī
Chouphala	Chouphalā
Chupatties	Chupātties
Dada	Dādā
Dhotar	Dhotār
Dinnanath	Dīnnanāth
Diwali	Diwālī
diwankhana	diwānkhānā
Dwarkabai	Dvārkābāi

Diacritics used in the First Edition

Gangabai	Gaṅgābāi
Ganpat Shantaram Vaidya	Ganpat Shāntārām Vaidyā
Ghanashampant	Ghanaśhāmpant
Harishchandra Sadashiva	Hariśchandra Sadāśiva
Hirabai	Hīrābāi
Hiroo	Hīroo
Kaka	Kākā
Kaki	Kākī
Kakubai	Kākubāi
Kamallabai	Kamalābāi
Kashinathpant	Kāśīnāthpant
khan	khān
Konkanastha	Koṇkanastha
Krishnabai	Kṛṣṇābāi
Kunku	Kunkū
mahera	māherā
mangalagauri	maṅgalagaurī
mangalsutra	maṅgalsūtra
mangalvar	maṅgalvār
Manjulabai	Manjulābāi
maravti	māravtī
mavashi	māvāshī
mavashis phule	māvāśī's phulè
mlench	mlenc
mughta	mughṭā
Muktabai	Muktābāi
Nagnath	Nāgnāth
Nagnathrav	Nāgnāthrāv
Nanibai	Nanībāi
Narayan	Nārāyaṇ
Narayanrao	Nārāyaṇrāo
padar	pādār
pan supari	pān supāri
panvida	pānviḍā
patal	pātal
pedhe	peḍhe
phani	phanī

phugadi	phugaḍi
pilao	pilāo
pilav	pilāv
Pratap Harischandra Khote	Pratap Hariśchandra Khotè
Prataprao	Pratāprāo
Rambhao	Rāmbhāo
Ratanbai	Ratanbāi
Ratna	Ratnā
sabhas	sabhās
Saheb	Sāheb
Sambare	Sambārè
sa-ri	sā-rī
sasubai	sasubāi
Shalu	Śālu
Shamrav	Śyāmrāo
Shantabai	Śāntābāi
Shanvar Vadha	Śānvar Vaḍhā
shastras	shāstrās
Shenvi	Shenvī
Shevantibai Nikambe	Shèvantibāi Nikambè
shloka	śloka
shravana	śrāvaṇa
sinhasta	sinhasta
Sittaram Krishnarav Sanzgiri	Sīttārām Kṛṣṇarav Sañjgiri
Sonabai	Sonābāi
Sovle	Sovlè
Stotra	Stotrā
Suna	Sunā
Tarabai	Tārābāi
Tat	ṭāṭ
Vada	Vādā
Vajantri	Vājantrī
Varana	Varaṇā
Vasudevrav Kashinath Dalvi	Vāsudevrāv Kāśīnāth Dalvī
Vati	Vāṭī
Vengurle	Vengurlè
Veni	Veṇī

Diacritics used in the First Edition

Veni phani	Veni phanī
Vihinbai	Vihinbāi
Vithaba	Viṭhabā
Vithabai	Vithabāi
Zach	Zac
Zhima	Zhīmā

AFTERWORD

In her Introduction, Chandani Lokugé makes a persuasive case for *Ratanbai* as a novel of social protest committed to exposing the adverse effects of restrictive orthodoxy on contemporary Indian womanhood. Lokugé also places the novel in its wider social context, showing how the form of the novel resembles a Bildungsroman. In this Afterword, I would like to return to the text by shifting the focus from the title to the subtitle of this novel, that is from *Ratanbai* to *A Sketch of a Bombay High Caste Hindu Young Wife*.

The word 'sketch' suggests something simple, rough, done rapidly, and without too much detail. The brevity of the novel and the bold strokes that mark its characterization certainly make it akin to a 'sketch'. The particularity of this sketch is also easily signified by the adjective 'Bombay'. Indeed, Ratanbai is very much a Bombay person, as much as she is an upper-caste Hindu and Marathi Brahmin. The city, which was the capital of the Presidency named after it, was fast becoming the leading centre of commerce and business in India, in addition to being the cultural and intellectual capital of western India. Bombay, like Calcutta and Madras, was a modern metropolis, a hotbed of social reform and political activism, where the 'New Woman' that Ratanbai is seeking to become, can actually be born.

But the other words in the 'High Caste Hindu Young Wife' invite closer scrutiny. This is because Ratanbai's specific caste and community are not emphasized. (From her pilgrimage to Goa and Sawantwadi, it is likely that she is a Shenvi, that is, a Saraswat Brahmin.) Instead, what is emphasized is her upper-caste, even Brahmin, identity as a *wife*. Hence, the novel records the merging, even metamorphosis, of such an identity with that of a modern Indian woman through the device of education. The multiple connotations and implications of the phrase 'young wife' have already been discussed by Lokugé. What interests me about the subtitle is that the other meaning of the word 'sketch'—which suggests description or representation—becomes crucial. The politics of representation in the novel forces us to question *what* is being represented and *how*.

The novel almost approximates an ethnographic study of the mores of upper-caste Hindus of the Bombay Presidency. Photographs inserted in the book together with their captions, certainly offer valuable clues about the intended audience of the book. Obviously, the book was actively encouraged, if not patronized, by the British colonial authorities. Not only is it dedicated to Queen Victoria, 'with profound gratitude and loyalty', but has a Preface by the wife of a former governor of Bombay Presidency, Ada Harris. In her own Preface, Nikambe praises Victoria's 'happy rule...brightening and enlightening the lives and homes of many Hindu women', thus asserting a causal (and beneficial) link between the reign of a woman monarch and her (Hindu) women subjects.

All these details confirm that the book was aimed, at least partially, at a British audience. On one hand, the novel not only documents the lives and times of a certain group of Indian women but seeks to validate it in the eyes of the British readers. This task is carried out systematically throughout the novel in detailed descriptions of dress, food, fasts, rituals, festivals, worship, pilgrimage, marriage, death, widowhood, and so on, thus providing a vivid picture of considerable sociological and historical value. Original Marathi and Sanskrit words are used all over the text; kinship relations, much more complicated in Hindu extended families, are neither 'translated' nor collapsed into simpler or generic English ones. Thus, the book attempts an 'authentic' representation. But, on the other hand, the book is also aimed at an Indian audience *through* a British one. The force and power of the patronage of the latter was intended to make the book acceptable to the former. *Ratanbai* thus performs a dual task: not only is it seeking to reform Hindu society by routing or legitimating itself via British colonial power, but also appealing and educating the latter to accept, even appreciate, the former.

The politics of such mediations, however, are determined by the unequal power relations between the ruled and the rulers. Indeed, the novel negotiates its way through several such unequal powers: men and women, Brahmins and non-Brahmins, upper-caste Hindus and lower-caste Hindus, and, perhaps, most importantly, educated and uneducated women. The last pair becomes, in this novel, the 'master' category, which in turn determines how all the rest are played out and arranged. What makes *Ratanbai* (and similar books like *Kamala* and *Saguna*) so remarkable is that they not only map the overlapping and contentious domains of caste, class, conversion, colonialism, and national consciousness, but that, ultimately, they are about the emergence of a new kind of subjectivity of a certain section of Indian women.

From the British side, such literature was useful in conveying the impression that the Raj was benign and beneficial to the natives. That is to say, the British ruled not so much through coercion but consent. It is clear that one such mask of conquest was the whole discourse of 'Improvement', which both the Liberals and Utilitarians employed to justify the empire. That the native elites also lent support to this imperial project by championing various kinds of social reform movements cannot be denied. But what is more important is that the motives of the two were far from identical. Reform, rather, was itself the contentious site where colonial domination and native resistance struggled for control and supremacy. Needless to say, there were no clear winners or losers, but what is clear is that the *interests* of the two, the colonized and the colonizers, were neither the same nor comfortably compatible with each

Afterword

other. The Indian reform project often ran afoul with imperial authority, increasingly so as the national struggle for liberation gathered force.

This ambivalence, which is typical to this day of the cultural economy of colonialism and postcolonialism, is also reflected in *Ratanbai*. This, to all appearances, is a single-issue novel, written almost as a propaganda tract to promote the education of upper-caste Hindu women. That the author herself ran such a school would suggest that she was not only well qualified to write on this topic, but was also promoting her own interests, howsoever indirectly. Nikambe's deferential seeking of patronage and her collusion with colonial power has already been discussed. Is the book, therefore, an opportunistic portrayal of the Hindu upper-caste woman so as to continue her subservience to colonial rule? Is such a 'sketch' an act of cultural perfidy or commerce? I would argue that just as collaboration with imperialism comes in various garbs, resistance too wears many guises—the masks of resistance are, in other words, as varied and heterogeneous as the masks of conquest. In *Ratanbai* too, the kowtowing to colonial power and paradigms might simultaneously indicate a more nuanced and ambivalent form of resistance.

At first we see little native resistance to colonialism in *Ratanbai*. On the contrary, it is as if Hindu traditions are coercive and colonial education liberative, if not lucrative. But such a picture is not sustained by a close reading of the text. Let us examine the only social encounter between Indians and the British, the party at Mrs B.'s that Lokugé has taken up in the Introduction. This event, unlike the later and invariably disastrous consequences of any social (or sexual) mixing of the races in later Anglo-Indian or Indian English literature, actually comes off rather well. Not only is this shown to be a pleasant and educative interaction but it passes without the least racial slur or insult. This is an instance of the socialization of Hindus so that they are turned into good and obedient subjects. But the rulers are also being made to understand that upper-caste Hindu women will continue to treat their rulers as outcastes, accepting only uncooked 'clean' food, such as fruit, from them. What is crucial here is native resistance, as much as the customary or 'orthodox' insistence on ritual purity.

Similarly, it might be argued that for upper-caste Hindu women, especially those who, like child-widows, were oppressed, conversion is recommended as a valuable, though not mandatory step in the 'right' direction. Nikambe was herself a convert to Christianity, but in her book she doesn't advocate such a recourse openly. There is the more subtle reference at the end of the novel to 'the Book'. This 'beautifully bound and gilt-edged Book' is seen as the real basis of the changed life of the protagonist and her husband. It is a book that both of them know and have accepted: 'we shall make it our guide in life'. However, this turning of the young couple from being people of rituals, superstitions, myths, and customs, so to speak, to people of the book is never highlighted, but quietly suggested at the end. In this respect, the novel suggests that it is education—and the whole transformation that it can bring about—that is non-negotiable: education, within Hinduism if possible, without Hinduism if necessary. This is quite different from some of the other conversion narratives of her time or missionary tracts that openly advocated conversion as the only way forward.

While conversion is not emphasized, the education of women is. That becomes, ostensibly, the single point and focus of the novel. If we were to ask the question, 'What does Rantanbai desire?' then the answer that the book proposes is most clearly 'education'. It is this singularity and clarity of purpose that makes Ratanbai a rather unique character in the annals of Indian literature. While desires are often confused and contradictory, and usually in conflict with a character's true self-interest, in this case there is neither contradiction, nor conflict, but a one-pointed consistency and reinforcement. Indeed, the difference between desire and interest is merged in the novel. The result is a remarkable eroticization of women's education, over all conflicting desires, including that of marital happiness or material well-being:

> How often, with an aching heart, she would sit dreaming about school life! Her teacher, her companions, her singing lesson, her English lesson, the

translation class, came before her, and then the longing would come, 'Oh! could I but go to school once again.'

While such pining, aching desire for school is likely to have few parallels in literature or life, it is not difficult to see how it echoes the passion of a character such as Jane Eyre to 'improve' herself and her prospects. Obviously, education is a metonym for *all* that an upper-caste Hindu woman of that time might desire, including equality, empowerment, security, and, above all, freedom, agency, autonomy, swaraj—to be in charge of one's own life, which is the promise that modernity brings with it. Education, then, stands for Indian modernity itself.

It is interesting that certain males are seen as primary proponents and supporters of this project, while certain women are seen as antagonists and obstructers. The battle of the sexes, therefore, has both men women pitted against their own ostensible interests! This not only goes to underscore the complexity of patriarchal social and gender relations during that period, but also suggests a different trajectory for Indian feminism. Ratanbai not only wins in the end, but her husband is also shown to be remarkably free of the kind of 'education envy' that has been characteristic of males in other cultural and discursive registers.

If an advocacy of women's education is the primary purpose of the novel, *Ratanbai* has also a secondary but equally important feature. One of the most dramatic and poignant episodes in the book, as Lokugé shows, is the sudden widowhood of Tarabai. It is here that Nikambe's two great themes come together. The treatment of the widowed Tara symbolizes all that is rotten in the life of upper-caste Hindu women. The antidote is what Ratanbai, and, later Tarabai, share—education. Both the problem and its solution are thus fused together to offer a coherent image of Indian modernity that the novel actually espouses.

The novel, ultimately, is not only an instantiation of empowerment and agency in that it was written by a woman for the welfare of her sisters, but also narrates and depicts such agency in its plot. Ratan may seem to be passive, requiring plot machinations to achieve what she wants, but I would like to offer an alternative reading. It is her intense *desire* for education that triumphs in the end; this desire or *iccha* is a sign of her will to power and therefore shows her as a strong and self-governed agent, endowed with Shakti—not a passive subject. Insofar as Ratan is native and colonized, the novel also shows the empowerment and will to freedom of other native and colonized people. Using a variety of stratagems and methods, such people will try to seize their destinies and struggle for a better way of life—in spite of colonialism, if not because of it.

That is possibly why *Ratanbai* does *not* problematize or interrogate several aspects of the society that it describes—not even the caste system—whose horrors are shown in one of its most moving scenes. Here, the utterly poor women of lower castes come for handouts even if the misfortunes of the rich are transferred to them with these gifts. Even of this horrid custom Nikambe astutely says that the poor did not share such beliefs and happily accepted what they could get. What we see, once again, is the adaptability of the native, her ability to survive in a situation of extreme duress. When it comes to her caste-sisters, Nikambe takes great pains, almost lovingly, to describe the integral features of their life including ceremonies such as *mangalagavri* and the ceremonial taking of each other's names by a married couple, and the *maher-sasar* politics.

Such descriptions bring me to the final point I wish to make about this *Sketch*. With its very imperative desire to record and, therefore, preserve for posterity a way of life, the novel suggests, in fact, a very clear understanding of the forces of history. Nikambe is well aware that she was living through times of tremendous change and transition and the Hindu society that she was picturing was fast changing before her very eyes. Her attempt to record, document, and even celebrate this way of life may not be signs of her conservativeness, but instead a subtle acknowledgement on her part that these ways were unsustainable under the onslaught of modernity. Indeed, at the end of the novel, not just Ratanbai, but even the widowed Tarabai, are educated, while Prataprao, Ratanbai's husband, has gone to England for higher studies and is about to return to India 'via

America, Japan, and China'—a rather circuitous route, but one which suggests a newly globally integrated family. Tarabai herself is no longer in widow's weeds, but in 'reformed' dress, with her hair grown back. She is said to look 'very sweet', and though she still does not wear *kunku* or ornaments, she dresses in a modern 'print jacket' and wears a shawl when outdoors. Thus, the five years that the narrative covers record changes that can be considered nothing short of revolutionary for a society such as the book describes.

The end of the novel, however, shows an idealized synthesis between forces of tradition and modernity, reform and conservation, Christianity and upper-caste Hindu ways, imperialism and national identity, women's emancipation/education and the continuation of patriarchal norms—all under the aegis of Queen Victoria's benign rule. Though such a dream was practically impossible, its eloquent narration reveals the author's longing to reconcile the contradictions of her times in a way that was most appealing to her.

Makarand Paranjape

EXPLANATORY NOTES

In compiling these notes, I have referred to the following: Allen, Michael, and S. N. Mukherjee, *Women in India and Nepal* (Delhi: Sterling Publishers, 1990); Athavale, Parvarti, *Hindu Widow: An Autobiography*, trans. Justin E. Abbott (1928, New Delhi: Reliance Publishing House, 1921); *Britannica 2001, Standard Edition CD-ROM*, (Chicago: Encyclopaedia Britannica, 2001); Burton, Antoinette, *At the Heart of the Empire: Indians and the Colonial Encounter in Late-Victorian Britain* (Berkeley: University of California Press, 1998); Case, Margaret H., *South Asian History 1750-1950: A Guide to Periodicals, Dissertations and Newspapers* (Princeton: Princeton University Press, 1968); Davenport, Adams, *Woman's Work and Work in Girlhood, Maidenhood and Wifehood* (London: John Hogg, 1880); Toru Dutt's letter to Miss Martin in 1876, in Harihar Das, *Life and Letters of Toru Dutt* (London: Oxford University Press, 1921); *Encyclopaedia of Asian Civilizations*, vol. 9, (Villecresnes: L. Frédéric, 1984); *Encyclopaedia Britannica* (1911); Forbes, Geraldine, *The New Cambridge History of India*, vol. no. 2, *Women in Modern India* (Cambridge: Cambridge University Press, 1996); Heimsath, Charles H., *Indian Nationalism and Hindu Social Reform* (Princeton: Princeton University Press, 1964, p. 153); Kosambi, Meera, 'Women's Emancipation and Equality: Pandita Ramabai's Contribution to Women's cause' in *Economics and Political Weekly*, 23, no. 44 (October 29), 1988; Kosambi, 'British Bombay and Marathi

Mumbai: Some Nineteenth Century Perceptions' in Sujata Patel and Alice Thorner (eds), *Bombay: Mosaic of Modern Culture* (Bombay; Delhi; Calcutta; Madras: Oxford University Press, 1995); Kumar, Radha, *The history of doing: an illustrated account of movements for women's rights and feminism in India, 1800–1990* (London; New York: Verso, 1993); Lahiri, Shompa, *Indians in Britain: Anglo-Indian Encounters, Race and Identity 1880–1930* (London: Frank Cass, 2000); Levine, Philippa, *Victorian Feminism 1850–1900* (London: Hutchinson, 1987); Luhrmann, T. M., *The Good Parsi: The Fate of a Colonial Elite in a Postcolonial Society*, (Cambridge; Massachusetts; London: Harvard University Press, 1996); MacMillan, Margaret, *Women of the Raj* (New York: Thames and Hudson, 1988); Mathur, Y. B., *Women's Education in India 1813–1966* (London: Asia Publishing House, 1973); Purvis, June, *A History of Women's Education in England* (Milton Keynes; Philadelphia: Open University Press, 1991); Ramabai, Pandita, *The High-Caste Hindu Woman* (1887; Bombay: Maharashtra State Board of Literature and Culture, 1981); *The Letters and Correspondence of Pandita Ramabai*, (ed.) A. B. Shah (Bombay: Maharashtra State Board of Literature and Culture, 1977); Ranade, Mrs Ramabai, *Himself, the Autobiography of a Hindu Lady*, trans. and adapt. by Katherine Van Akin Gates (New York: Longman, Green and Co., 1938); Reddy, S. Muthulakshmi, *Autobiography of Dr (Mrs) Muthulakshmi Reddy* (n.d.); Riddick, John F., *Who was Who in British India* (Westport, Conn.; London: Greenwood Press, 1998); Satthianadhan, Krupabai, *Saguna: the First Autobiographical Novel in English by an Indian Woman* (New Delhi: Oxford University Press, 1998); Satthianadhan, *Kamala: The Story of a Hindu Wife* (New Delhi: Oxford University Press, 1998); Satthianadhan, *Miscellaneous Writings* (Madras: Srinivasa, Varadachari and Co., 1896); Sorabji, Cornelia, *India Calling: The Memories of Cornelia Sorabji, India's First Woman Barrister* (New Delhi: Oxford University Press, 2002); Sorabji, *Love and Life Behind the Purdah* (New Delhi: Oxford University Press, 2003); Taylor, Jane and Ann Taylor, *Little Ann and Other Poems* (London and New York: George Routledge & Sons, 1883); *The New Encyclopaedia Britannica*, vol. 2 (Chicago: Encyclopaedia Britannica, c. 1994); *The Oxford English Dictionary, Second Ed.* (Oxford: Clarendon Press, 1989); *The Poetical Works of Felicia Dorothea Hemans* (Oxford: Oxford University Press, 1914); Vicinus, Martha, *Suffer and Be Still: Women in the Victorian Age* (Bloomington: Indian University Press, 1972).

The notes refer to the page numbers in the text. I have included in these notes, local words, mainly Marathi, which were not footnoted in the first edition, and which could be considered significant to the reading of the text.

NOTE ON THE TEXT

viii *Marshall Brothers, London*: Some of their late nineteenth-century titles included: Charles Bartholemew, *A Lecture on Turkish Baths* (1886); John Urquhart, *Modern Discoveries and the Bible* (1898); Irene Barnes, *Behind the Pardah: The Story of C.E.Z.M.S. Work in India* (1899).

DEDICATION

3 *Queen, Empress of India*: Queen Victoria (1819–1901). Queen of Great Britain and Ireland from 1837–1901. She was proclaimed 'Empress of India' by the Royal Titles Act of 1876, emphasizing and consolidating British dominance of the subcontinent. The word 'imperialism' was coined in the late 1870s to explain the process. Queen Victoria's Diamond Jubilee of 1897 marked the high tide of the British Empire.

PREFACE

7 *Lady Harris*: Lucy Ada Jervis, born 29 October 1851. Second daughter of Carnegie Robert John Jervis, third Viscount St Vincent of Meaford by Lucy Charlotte, daughter of John Baskervyle-Glegg. Married George Robert Canning Harris, fourth Baron Harris at Godmersham, Kent, on 8 July 1874. Lord Harris was

governor of Bombay from 1890–5. Lady Ada Harris accompanied her husband to Bombay, where she visited Shevantibai Nikambe's school. Lady Ada Harris died on 12 February 1930.

high caste: According to the *Varna* (Hindu caste system), Hindus are born into one of the four castes which are, in order of diminishing prestige, the *Brahmins*, the spiritual governors and heads of society, and originally scholars and priests; the *Kshatriyas*, warriors, and often, as a result of their skills in conquest or a reward for success, rulers and landowners; *Vaishyas*, usually businessmen, traders, artisans; and *Sudras*, usually the peasants, though not all peasants are *Sudras*.

early marriages: Before c. 400BC, Hindu girls could remain unmarried until about sixteen years of age and could select their own partners. The institution of child marriage was introduced in India in c. 300 BC, necessitating the introduction of arranged marriages. Child marriage gradually gained popularity and became obligatory from c. 200 BC. It was considered a religious and social obligation among the higher castes, and parents faced religious and social ostracism if they did not comply with it. According to the *Dharma Shastra* of Vyasa: 'The sin incidental to an act of procuring an abortion is committed, if through the negligence of her giver (the father), a girl menstruates before her marriage.' Parents arranged early alliances for their daughters because of competition for eligible marriage partners. Since a wife was compelled to live with her husband's family, the groom's parents often desired a daughter-in-law young enough to adjust to her new domestic surrounding.

In the nineteenth century, child marriage was practised in all parts of India. Girls were often betrothed in their infancy. Five to eleven years was the usual period for Brahmins. In 1860, the age of marriage for girls was raised to ten years, and in 1891 to twelve years. However, the Age of Consent Bill enraged orthodox Hindus who felt that it sullied the 'ancient glory' of India, and the practice of child marriage continued almost unabated. See Ranade, *Himself, the Autobiography*; Athavale, *Hindu Widow, An Autobiography*; Toru Dutt's letter to Miss Martin in 1876, in Das, *Life and Letters of Toru Dutt*, p. 248; Heimsath, *Indian Nationalism*, p. 153.

advantages of education: Late nineteenth-century British reformers often referred to the 'degraded' status of women within Indian cultures as a justification for the inevitability of British rule. They aimed to modernize India to British standards and improve the status of women through appropriate education for both sexes. The progress of female literacy in India was slow until the late nineteenth century, hampered by inconsistent government policy, lack of resources and opposition from orthodox religious groups. Education for girls did not automatically enhance the prestige and financial success of Indian families in the same way as education for boys. Many superstitions abounded about the consequences of female education, including the belief that a literate wife was immoral and portended danger, or even death, to her husband. Furthermore, in a region where sexual segregation was the norm, girls had to have their own schools if they were to be allowed to go out of their home.

In the early nineteenth century, girls' schools were mostly funded privately by missionaries in India. The Act of 1813 provided that a lakh of rupees be annually 'set apart and applied to the revival and improvement of literature and the encouragement of the learned Natives of India and for the introduction and promotion of a knowledge of the sciences among the inhabitants of the British Territories in India'. After ten years, a Committee of Public Instruction was set up to encourage ancient learning, the modern sciences, and the teaching of English. However, Thomas Babbington Macaulay's famous*Minute on Education* (1835) set a new trend that favoured western education in English.

Until 1854, government resources were mostly directed towards the education of Indian boys. However, government policy changed with Sir Charles Wood's educational dispatch of 1854, which detailed the need for mass education in the vernacular for both sexes as well as higher education for elite castes. At the same time, female education began to gain support among Indians who wanted social and religious reform, or recognized opportunities for social and financial mobility. The number of girls' schools expanded rapidly. These included government schools and schools sponsored by reformist religious organizations such as the Brahmo Samaj, the Prarthana Samaj, Arya Samaj, and Theosophical Society. See also n. 7, *Students' Literary and Scientific Society*, and Cornelia Sorabji, *India Calling* n. 11-12, pp. 221-3.

In 1854, Bombay had sixty-five girls' schools out of a national total of 626. During the last two decades of the nineteenth century, demand increased substantially for female education in India, leading to a marked expansion in rates of female literacy. From 1886-1901 the total number of girl students in India rose from 2,14,206 to 3,44,712. Although boys still outnumbered girls by nine to one, this was double the rate of increase among male students. Despite these achievements, at only 2.49 per cent of the female population, attendance rates in Indian girls' schools remained low in comparison to England, where universal elementary education had been introduced through the Elementary Education Act of 1870. Although school attendance in England and Wales was initially at the discretion of local school boards, the Act of 1880 ensured that elementary school attendance became compulsory for both sexes to the age of ten years. The minimum age requirement was raised to eleven years in 1893, and fourteen in 1899.

Compared to Parsees (also spelt Parsis) and Muslims, Hindus in Bombay were comparatively slow to take advantage of new female educational facilities, which included secondary and teacher training schools, as well as arts and science colleges. Although only six women attended Indian universities during 1881–2, by the end of the century there were 264. During these years, girls' secondary school enrolments increased twentyfold to 41,582. As western-educated husbands and fathers abandoned customs such as child marriage, education became more accessible for Indian girls.

7 *Native schools*: See n. 7, *decent education*.

Students' Literary and Scientific Society: An influential, reforming organization, founded in 1849 by Professor Patton of Elphinstone College, Bombay. Like other liberal British educators of the period, Patton encouraged Indian people to organize their own female education on a secular basis. The society was initially patronized by both the staff and students of Elphinstone, which was the first college of higher education based on the western model in the Bombay Presidency. After 1857, its membership expanded to Bombay University. Many of its key male members pursued educational reforms, particularly the spread of female education and the establishment of new girls' schools.

decent education after they were married: Early marriages curtailed the freedom of most girls to attend schools. Although education was beginning to be included in English-speaking Indian definitions of the 'perfect lady'[1], Hindu wives, like their British counterparts, were expected to continue in their supportive role to their husband and extended family. Consequently, household and maternal duties interfered with school attendance and study habits. Often the strongest protest against women's education came from the women themselves. The custom of purdah (seclusion of women in high-caste families), made it almost

---

[1] For information about the Victorian New Woman- image of the Perfect Lady, see for instance, Vicinus, *Suffer and Be Still*; Levine, *Victorian Feminism*; Davenport, *Woman's Work*. For information on Indian New Woman ideologies, see Forbes, *The New Cambridge History*, pp. 28–9.

impossible for the wives to leave home to attend school. Brahmins also feared 'pollution' from pork and beef eaters in government and mission schools, where religions, castes, and sexes were often mixed. In the late nineteenth century, as demand increased for female education, there was also a chronic shortage of female teachers. Among the upper castes, western-educated men often took it upon themselves to pass on literacy and English-language skills to their wives and daughters, or engaged tutors at home. Also during this period, some missionary schools began to cater exclusively to the customary needs of high-caste Hindu girls. See Ranade, *Himself, the Autobiography*; Satthianadhan, *Saguna*, pp. 137–8.

8 *not too engrossing*: See n. 7 *decent education after they were married*. Despite its importance as a modernizing influence, female education was not intended to interfere with household and family duties. Generally, British wives were equally restricted in their intellectual pursuits by the expectation that their role was that of the 'selfless helpmate'. See MacMillan, *Women of the Raj*, pp. 119, 201.

9 *Her Majesty, whose happy rule in my dear native land*: Nikambe was not alone in her enthusiasm for British rule. Other prominent female social reformers of the time expressed similar pro-colonial sentiments in acknowledgment of the modernizing influence of British rule on status of women in India. See for instance, Ramabai, *The High Caste Hindu Woman*; Sorabji, *India Calling*; Satthianadhan, *Miscellaneous Writings*.

the late Governor of Bombay: Fourth Baron, Lord George Robert Canning Harris, ex-Governor of Bombay (1890–5). Born 3 February 1851 at St Ann's, Trinidad. Son of George Frances Robert Harris, third Lord Harris and Sarah Cummins. Educated at Eton and Christ Church, Oxford. Married Lucy Ada Jervis in 1874. The Harris family's link with India can be traced back to 1788, when the first Lord Harris received a military assignment in

Bombay. Before being appointed Governor of Bombay, Lord George Harris held the posts of Under-Secretary of State for India (1885–6) and Under-Secretary of State for War (1886–9). He is remembered principally for his exceptional ability as an international test match cricket captain and for popularizing cricket in Bombay. Lord George Harris died on 24 March 1932 in Kent.

Bombay: British India consisted of the three old Presidencies of Madras, Bengal, and Bombay.

Although India did not come under British government rule until 1858, the East India Company ran Bombay as a British territory from 1668. (It was ceded to King Charles II in 1661 by the Portuguese as part of his marriage settlement). At that time, Bombay consisted of seven separate small islands. During the nineteenth century, the city of Bombay spread via causeways and land reclamation projects to join all the islands together to form a single Bombay island, later expanding in the twentieth century to the mainland or Konkan Coast. Its rapid growth signified a major geographical shift as a power centre after the British defeated the Maratha ruler, the Peshwa of Poona, in 1818. As the capital city of the Bombay Presidency, and India's major western seaport, Bombay was of major socio-cultural and economic importance to the British Empire, and prospered after the opening of the Suez Canal in 1869.

British-Indian contact was felt equally strongly in the British provinces of Bombay, Bengal, and Madras. Common to all the Presidencies was Indian women's reform. However in Bombay, important specificities within the Hindu class structure directly affected these reforms. The body of Hindu reformers who emerged in western India were in the main elitist Brahmins (unlike in Bengal, for instance, where many upper castes dominated the social structure). Thus, colonialist reforms worked most effectively in collaboration with traditional elitist-religious and socio-cultural ideologies. In education, for instance, Mountstuart Elphinstone, Governor of Bombay

(1819–27), and the first British Commissioner of the Deccan, introduced the *dakshina* system in Hindu College, Poona, which trained Brahmin students in classical Sanskrit studies before gradually introducing them to western science and philosophy. The introduction of widow remarriage was another important strategy of the social reform movement in Bombay in the 1860s. As in educational reforms, the reformers sought to initiate change through traditional social channels prevalent in the Brahmin structure of the area. See also Chaudhuri, *Indian Women's Movement: Reform and Revival* (Delhi: Sangam Books, 1993), pp. 29–35.

her deep interest in India's women: Although the British Government discouraged British interference in Indian customs after the Indian Mutiny of 1857, the wives of viceroys and governors were exempted from conventional codes of female behaviour due to their status. Consequently, it was easier for them to influence policy in relation to Indian women. See n. 8, *not too engrossing*. *Miss Manning*: Probably Elizabeth Adelaide Manning (1828–1905[?]), Hon Secretary of the National India Association (founded 1877), which was committed to promoting knowledge about India, furthering understanding between Indians and the British, and non-interference in Indian social and religious customs. Manning travelled to Bombay in 1888, and was an early patron of Cornelia Sorabji, India's first woman student to graduate from Bombay University. See also, Sorabji, *India Calling*, p. ix, and n. 44, p. 239.

CHAPTER I

11   *Ratanbai*: *Bai* translates as the Mrs or Miss suffix to a woman's name. *Rao*, *Ji*, and *Pant* all translate as Mr when added to men's names. It is interesting that Nikambe always refers to the westernized Vasudevrav as Mr, while all the women retain *bai* attached to their names.

High Court: The Bombay High Court was constructed in 1878 in the city's Fort area.

12 *mangalsutra*: The wedding symbol. Jewellery has perennially decorated Hindu males and females, but females particularly attached great importance to it. For, although the orthodox Hindu woman was entitled to various rights to inherited property like *stridhana* (dowry), she was often unable to enforce these rights due to the patriarchy's refusal to recognize them. In reality, jewellery provided her only means to independence (unless it was stolen from her by mercenary in-laws). Parents who were sensitive to this issue made sure their daughter had a good portion of jewellery at the time of her marriage. See for instance, Satthianadhan, *Kamala*, p. 162.

clerks who squatted on the floor: Although this was customary practice, the lower professional and social status of the clerks is also designated by the fact that they do not use the British-style chairs and tables as part of their work practice.

fair complexion: Light or pale complexion. Always a positive physical attribute that figures strongly in the selection of a bride in India. Fair is synonymous with beauty.

uneducated family: Here the author follows British colonialist notions in which uneducated meant without western education. Prior to British rule, education in the Indian subcontinent consisted of religious instruction. Indian women's education reached its lowest ebb in the late eighteenth and nineteenth centuries. Although females of the Vedic period had access to traditional religious education, even to the highest knowledge of the Absolute or *Brahma*, the ensuing Brahminical social order gradually lowered the familial and social status of women, denying them access to education. Further restrictions took place as child marriage gained popularity. During the nineteenth century, the orthodox Hindu girl's training consisted of domestic activities in the women's quarters, and generally comprised role-indoctrination in *pativratadharma* (husband-worship), which was believed to be the source of female spiritual liberation or moksha. She was also instructed in religious and secular literatures and in popular socio-religious beliefs by the elder members of her own as well as her husband's family. See also n. 7, *advantages of education*.

the promise was made by the mother: Reference to arranged infant or child marriage.

13 *college*: Identified later in *Ratanbai* (p. 45) as Wilson College in Bombay, which was founded by a British missionary, the Rev. Dr John Wilson, as an elementary school in 1832. The present Wilson College was completed on a new site around 1887. It held the reputation of being one of the premier boys' school for high-caste Indians in Bombay.

breakfast: To avoid cooking in the midday heat, breakfast and dinner were the major meals of the day. Breakfast commonly consisted of a cooked meal of breads, vegetable dishes, and chutneys. It was mostly eaten between 9–11 a.m. The working day usually began long before this, at dawn.

The dining room was dismal looking: The westernized (rather censorious) authorial point of view is transparently revealed. Traditional Hindu homes were customarily furnished sparingly and were more utilitarian than decorative, possibly because of the emphasis placed on spiritual life.

the sacred thread: A white cord worn continuously by Hindu males after formal initiation into Brahmin or Kshastriya castes (See n. 7 *high caste*) between the ages of seven and twelve. It is generally worn draped diagonally across the shoulder and round the waist. In this rite, a Hindu is 'twice born' or *dvija*.

head is shaved: Customary for orthodox Hindu males.

modestly: An important wifely attribute connected to her traditional role of *pativrata*. See n. 12, *uneducated family*.

alone and in silence, devours his fresh hot breakfast: An orthodox Hindu wife never accompanied her husband at meals. She generally stood aside to serve him. She was also expected to undergo 'a bath of ceremonial purity' before preparing and serving the food, not only to the husband, but to the elder women of the household. See also, Ranade, *Himself*, pp. 114, 209.

14 *boots*: A British innovation.

landau: A four-wheeled horse-drawn carriage with a top that opens into two folding hoods over the passenger compartment. When open, the rear part is folded back, while the front part is removed entirely. It was named after the German town where the vehicle was first made.

the servant...made calls on his friends, and had a short smoke and nap before returning home: The privileged status of the household is indicated by the minimal duties of its servants.

III. Standard Class: The lesson books used by European missionary contained elementary geography and history in the vernacular tongues, a selection from Indian books describing ideas about duty, and excerpts from the scriptures setting out the basic system of Christian ethics. In the 1893 syllabus, *Royal Readers* I–IV were prescribed as English textbooks from lower primary (Standard I) to middle (Standard VII) levels in girls' schools and zenanas in Calcutta. See Kumar, *The History of Doing*, p. 16.

sari: Traditional attire for Hindu women. Generally, six yards of cloth are draped around the body, from the waist down, with one end draped across the *choli* (blouse) and over the left shoulder. The draping varies with race and caste.

Casabianca: Romantic poem by Hemans (1793–1835). More commonly recognized by its first line: 'The boy stood on the burning deck.' The literal translation of Casabianca's name (white house) gives a clue to his moral status as an honorary white, despite his 'exotic' oriental patrimony as the son of an Egyptian 'chieftain'. Casabianca is a boy of about thirteen years of age when his father's ship catches fire during the Battle of the Nile. In this tragic poem, Casabianca heroically refuses to leave his post on the burning ship without his father's permission, unaware that his father is already dead. The boy perishes as the ship continues to be bombarded by cannon fire, upholding the honour of his father and ensuring his own prestige as an obedient son and national hero. See Hemans, *The Poetical Works*, p. 396.

16 *The chairs, sofas, and tables were moved into another room...Hindu ladies...were seated in groups on the carpet*: Generally, Hindu religious ceremonies are conducted with the guests seated at a lower level to the positioning of the gods on a platform or table.

18 *already educated in the old style*: Contrary to her earlier comment about 'uneducated' families, Nikambe concedes that training females in orthodox Hindu scriptures, customs, and values did represent another form of education. Compare n. 12, *uneducated family*.

averse to 'new or reformed ideas': See 'Introduction', p. xix.

Her duty was to please, and to be most obedient: Generally, Hindu child-wives left parental homes, sometimes at puberty, sometimes earlier, to live with the husband's family if the husband or mother-in-law so desired. A wife returned to her own home only for occasional short visits. Until she attained motherhood, a child-wife was entirely dependent upon her mother-in-law and other elder persons in her husband's household. Her training in wifely and housewifely duties and religious practices, initiated by her mother, was continued by her mother-in-law. Under the government of ignorant mothers-in-law, the child-wife's life could turn into real drudgery. See Devi, *Amar Jiban*; Ramabai, *Himself*; Reddy, *Autobiography*; Satthianadhan, *Kamala*. The fact that Ratan is allowed much more flexibility in visiting her in-laws shows the western influence infiltrating her own home as well as that of the in-laws'.

20 *Shloka*: Verses.

hack victoria: Hired carriage of the type known as a victoria; a light, low, four-wheeled horse-drawn carriage with a folding hood, two passenger seats, and an elevated seat in the front for the driver.

Benares: Also spelt Banares, but currently known as Varanasi. It is one of the seven sacred cities of India, and dedicated to the cult of Siva. At the beginning of the seventeenth century, the city had more than 1500 temples, but most were destroyed during hostilities towards the end of that century. Millions of pilgrims visit its river ghats (stepped banks) each year to wash away their sins or scatter the ashes of relatives over the sacred waters.

dressed in pure white... Her head was shaved: The white sari and tonsure are symbolic of withdrawal into celibacy and asceticism. Both are compulsory for Hindu widows.

21 *'Hindu Club'*: There were Hindu, Muslim, and Parsee clubs and gymkhanas in Bombay and other Indian metros at the time. They were modelled on the clubs that the English set up in India; however, the latter were usually for whites only. Similarly, the native clubs functioned on 'communal' lines.

CHAPTER II

25 *Bai Saheb*: term of respect.

the letters and the address were like Greek to them: The telegram incident succinctly illustrates the problems of female illiteracy.

26 *Oh! do not make his wife a widow*: Although widow remarriage was practised in ancient India, the custom gradually became unpopular among the high-caste and upper-class Hindus. A Hindu widow was obliged to withdraw from the world and devote her life to celibacy, asceticism and worship of gods—Siva and her dead

husband—to assist in the spiritual liberation of her husband. By the nineteenth century the institutionalized restrictions on widowhood were considerable. Economically, a widow was entirely dependent on the joint family. Hindu widowhood also carried social stigma: a widow was an outcast who had no personal rights and was abused as a harbinger of ill luck. A husband's death could be directly attributed to his wife's perceived misconduct. See also *Himself*, p. xii: 'as a punishment for the sin which was responsible for the death of her husband, she (the widow) must remain forever a widow'.

The wretch has swallowed our Dinu: See n. 26, *Oh! do not make his wife a widow*.

The light—the god of her life—was no more. 'What is the use of living!' thought she. For Hindu wives, spiritual liberation could only be achieved through *pativratadharma* (husband-worship).

27 *government high school*: Government high schools generally enrolled both sexes, and provided an education on more traditional curricular lines, emphasizing the Hindu classics and scriptures. The western curriculum was introduced gradually and indirectly. Mountstuart Elphinstone provided the impetus for this development by promoting the publication of scientific and grammatical texts in the Marathi language (spoken by 50 per cent of Bombay's population) for the Elphinstone Institution. This inspired the opening of Marathi-language government schools. See also, n. 9, *Bombay*.

Nasik: Inland town about 150 km north-east of Bombay, which was located in the Deccan region of the Bombay Presidency during the nineteenth century. With over 300 temples, Nasik is a place of pilgrimage for Hindus.

The Konkan: The mainland coastal area adjacent to Bombay island.

28 *The poor girl widow could not be sent to her mother*: The stigma attached to widowhood would make life even more miserable for a widow if she resided in a place where

the people were 'very bigotted and foolish'.
Ratanbai, who no longer belonged to her own family: See n. 18, *her duty was to please.*
Her young widowed aunt had touched her: Kakubai's callousness is in marked contrast to Ratanbai's compassion. Perhaps the author wishes us to attribute this to her British-style education, youth, or her married status outside the family.

30 *These two always had food that was specially prepared for them*: While the head of the household always had meals specially prepared and served, widows were required to cook their own food which only they could consume, alone, once a day. It is interesting that the widow Kaku seems not to be bound by this custom.
She herself had her meals last of all, afterwards: See n. 13, *alone and in silence.*
cleaned grain by grain: Unpolished rice required meticulous time-consuming cleaning to separate it from grit and small stones. (An aside: Indian women often held a low opinion of the 'shortcuts' taken by British women in purchasing ground flours and other prepared food.) See Margaret MacMillan, *Women of the Raj*, p. 143.

CHAPTER III

32 *do not touch anything else*: Reference to the Brahmin belief that physical contact with food handled by foreigners (who were without a Hindu caste) would mean moral pollution and loss of caste to Brahmins. If polluted, Brahmins had to undergo a process of purification. According to MacMillan (*Women of the Raj*, pp. 58–60), this was a considerable source of irritation to the British in India, who had been brought up to show their hospitality by sharing food and resented 'being lumped together with sweepers and other Untouchables'. The British doubted whether there could be social intercourse between cultures when religious orthodoxies and local customs prevented

Indian women from attending British dinner parties for fear of pollution.
allowing her no extra jewels except a nose ring: Possibly because Ratanbai would be alone and unattended at this particular party, and the mother feared theft.
Malabar Hill: Old Bombay city's highest point at the end of the western hills, overlooking the financial district. By the second half of the nineteenth century, Malabar Hill was one of Bombay's most affluent and fashionable suburbs. The area was named after the Malabaris from the south-west coastal city of Malabar. During Portuguese rule (1534–1661), migrant Malabaris used the hill as a lookout for European merchant ships that could be plundered for treasure.

33 *each of us had a veni given her*: Gifts of flower wreaths were a British concession to local custom.
Diwankhana: lounge or drawing room.
pumbalows: a fruit that tastes like sweet line.

34 *Balajipant was there to serve, so it was a regular Hindu repast*: Emphasizing that the girls would not be polluted. Generally, the poorer Brahmins often worked for Europeans as gardeners, but did not work as cooks due to the risk of pollution from European foods.
we were taken outside to the pipe, and Balajipant gave us water: See n. 32, *do not touch anything else*. By drinking straight from the pipe, the girls would not risk exposure to 'polluted' water handled by foreigners. In the late nineteenth century, Malabar Hills gained its own reservoir. Piped water was an indicator of the high economic status in a household.
Thimble: Most likely to be a popular British game that required one child to hide a thimble and the others to search for it. Each finder took a turn at hiding the thimble.
Meddlesome Matty: Poem by Ann Taylor (1782–1866). A cautionary tale of the uncomfortable consequences of curiosity; in this case, the physical pain suffered by Matty

when she pries into her grandmother's snuff box. The poem was published in Jane Taylor and Ann Taylor, *Little Ann and Other Poems* (London and New York: George Routledge & Sons, 1883) pp. 25-7.

the Queen's stotra: Originally translated as the Queen's hymn but most likely to mean anthem.

35 *punkahs*: Fans. Could be portable and made from a palmyra leaf, or a large swinging cloth on a frame worked manually by coolies, who kept the punkah in motion by pulling rhythmically on a cord. In Bombay, punkahs were also made of polished wood.

our Aryanism is getting all defiled: Reiterates the orthodox Hindu community's veneration of Aryanism. Particularly because of colonialist reforms, traditionalists placed high moral value on racial purity. Ironically, Hindu reformers also used Aryanism to support their case. See 'Introduction', pp. xxiii-xxiv.

Are not they incarnations of monkeys?: Kakubai's racial prejudice reverses British prejudices about Asians by depicting the British as uncivilized and bestial. Paradoxically, the British discovery that Indians were largely Aryan, like themselves, led to their rulers to conclude that the British had a duty to civilize Indians to their own standards. See MacMillan, *Women of the Raj*, p. 58.

shravana: Festival held in the rainy season during which Lord Shiva, his consort Parvati and their son, Lord Ganesha are popularly worshipped.

36 *so as not to touch the woman*: A pollution taboo. Members of the Brahmin caste believe that they will be morally polluted if they touch a person of low caste. See also n. 32, *do not touch anything else*.

all the abuse, the misery, and unhappiness of the family would rest on this woman: The act of giving alms to the poor is framed in terms of personal gain for the giver (emotional peace and happiness). See also Paranjape, 'Afterword'.

Shastras: Hindu scriptures.

Explanatory Notes

37   *mangalwar*: Means Tuesday, considered auspicious to worship Lord Hanuman who assisted Lord Rama in the great epic *Ramayana* to defeat the demon king Ravana and rescue Sita, the consort of Rama. Devotees worship Hanuman every Tuesday so that any obstructions or impediments can be avoided or diverted.
Walkeshwar: Bombay suburb.
puja: prayer ceremony.

38   *'reformed' party*: In this instance, Hindu supporters of female education. See also 'Introduction', pp. xxi–xxii.

39   *happy news to all*: Sons were celebrated in Hindu families by both parents. A son was his mother's sole provider in her old age and, according to Hindu scripture, his father's spiritual saviour. In western India, elders and priests may bless a woman with the words 'Mayest thou have eight sons...' Religion sanctioned a husband's right to remarry after the eleventh year of marriage if his wife bore him no sons.

40   *Goa*: Major port and small state on the west coast of India, about 400 km south of Bombay. Important for both its Hindu temples and Christian churches, which were founded during Portuguese rule.

41   *Vengurle*: Vengurla, a west-coast port located near the north border of Goa province.
The ground served instead for everything: The contrast in living style indicates the comparative lack of British influence outside metropolitan Bombay.

42   *Sawantwadi*: Also spelt *Savantvadi* and *Savantwadi*. A city located about forty kilometres inland from the port of Vengurla. Formerly a small state ruled by the ancient royal lineage of Savantwadi, the Bhonsle family. After the area ceded to the East India Company in 1819, its rulers embraced a British-influenced development programme. By the turn of the twentieth century, Savantwadi was recognized as a model state.
Kolapur: Kolhapur. Prior to British Residency, Kolhapur was a small Maratha state that had been weakened by

persistent Moghul invasions. Its ancient city is located about 300 km south-east of Bombay. The city is a sacred place for Hindus, containing many temples such as the ninth-century temple of Mahalakshmi.

Vada: Palace. Possibly the New Palace at Kolhapur built towards the end of the nineteenth century. British Residency was forcefully established in Kolhapur during 1844–8, with the result that unhappy Kolhapur troops joined the Indian Mutiny of 1857. Afterwards, the British invested great care and attention in the western-style education of two Kolhapur heirs and their descendants. The effects of this policy became noticeable in 1894 when Shahu Chhatrapati came to the throne and embarked on a British-influenced programme of social reform and public building.

43 *I wish I had known how to converse in English*: Ratanbai acknowledges that her education will be inadequate unless she is able to hold a conversation in English. According to Mathur, 'The introduction of English into schools, particularly after 1835, created a cleavage between the intelligentsia and the rest of the people, because the former were enlightened in a culture that was unknown to the others.' See *Women's Education in India*, p. 26. A pass in English was obligatory for the successful completion of matriculation examinations for university entrance. See Sorabji, *India Calling*, n. 23, p. 230.

She did attend to the household duties… but, literally, her day was mostly spent doing nothing: Nikambe's idea of 'doing nothing' generally means without any intellectual work.

45 *Wilson College*: See n. 13, *college*.

bikbali: A jewelled ornament.

Bombay University: One of the three western-modelled universities that were founded in India in 1857.

46 *If some lady were to open a class for the married ladies, I would be the first one to send Anandi*: This is somewhat contradictory as Vasudevrav's married daughter, Ratan, does attend school. He possibly means schools set up

exclusively for older high-caste Hindu wives. By the end of the nineteenth century, western-educated Indian men were beginning to realize that an educated wife was an important career asset. Since the British clearly viewed the appearance of Indian wives at public meetings as a sign of social progress in India, they favoured groups that encouraged the presence of women at their gatherings. See Allen and Mukherjee, *Women in India and Nepal*, p. 113. Ramabai Ranade also records that her husband, Bombay High Court judge, Justice Madhav Govind Ranade, frequently insisted that she accompanied him to public meetings when she would rather have stayed at home. He also encouraged her to speak at public events. See *Himself*, pp. 22, 36–7.

50 *Pray to the gods, go to the temples and pay the vows, that he may have success*: Orthodox Hindus recognized that an intellectual woman posed a threat to the status quo. Prataprao's failure seems to confirm that threat. His family concludes that social order can only be restored if Ratanbai does penance through prayer for usurping his role.

Bandora: Probably Bandra, on the west coast of Salsette, to the north of Bombay island.

51 *in spite of the hateful remarks of the caste brethren*: This provides a clearer and less personal reason for Ratan's mother-in-law's reluctance to allow the girl to attend school. In the nineteenth century, Hindu families were under strong social pressure from their caste to resist the trend for educating girls at school. See n. 12, *uneducated family*.

Times of India: National English-language newspaper, published simultaneously in Bombay and Delhi. Launched in 1861, the *Times of India* merged two former Bombay newspapers: the *Bombay Times and Standard* (1859–61) and the *Bombay Telegraph and Courier* (1847–61).

the name, which according to custom, never passed her lips except in a song or rhyme: Traditionally, a Hindu woman was taught to respect her husband by avoiding any use of his first name. This is indicated by the various methods that women devised to refer to their husbands when writing their autobiographies. For instance, Ramabai Ranade referred to her husband as 'himself'; Parvatibai Karve used the respectful plural 'our men'; while Lakshmibai Tilak and Anandibai Karve referred to their husbands by their surnames. See Kosambi, 'Women Emancipation and Equality,' p. 49.

encouraged him to go to England: Prataprao's parents' religious conservatism is, in this instance, secondary to their more utilitarian desire for him to succeed among a government-employed professional Indian elite. Under government policy dating from c. 1840s, qualified English-educated Indian men would, in theory, be given preference in government appointments. But until 1922, all Indian Civil Service (ICS) examinations were held in London. The entry requirements were stringent: Indian candidates were required to spend one to two probationary years at a major British University such as London, Oxford or Cambridge, with compulsory residence being introduced in 1876. In practice, this prevented most Indians from being admitted to the ICS.

53 *listen to the novels*: Since the women were not literate in English, the word 'novel' could not refer to the English novel. It possibly refers to the Hindu classics.

54 *looking at the gardener with an evil eye*: See n. 12, *uneducated family*.

55 *the funeral was attended by six hundred gentlemen*: It was not a ritual that required women in attendance.

devotedly and faithfully filled her position as wife, mother and sister: Anandibai is remembered as an exemplary wife (devoted and faithful in the tradition of *pativrata*) although she has not provided the intellectual companionship that her husband desired. See n. 46, *If some lady were to open a class for married ladies.*

you have been the cause of our misery: See n. 26, *Oh! do not make his wife a widow.*

56 *a Hindu reformer*: See n. 18, *averse to 'new or reformed ideas'*.
Tara's very appearance betrayed that she was a girl widow: An orthodox Hindu widow was required to surrender any form of adornment, to shave her head, and dress in white.
Widows' Home: Possibly Sharada Sadan. Social reformer and Christian convert, Pandita Ramabai, established the first school for widows, Sharada Sadan, in Bombay in 1889. It attempted to observe Brahmin caste rules while maintaining a policy of non-sectarianism. Financial problems and strong criticism from orthodox Hindus caused the school to move to Poona, the next year. Although some girls were initially withdrawn after allegations that Ramabai was converting women to Christianity, by 1900 the Sharada Sadan had trained eighty widows to take up work as teachers or nurses.

Ramabai's work was furthered through a number of women who were influenced by her: for example, Shevantibai Nikambe, of course; and Godubai Joshi (later Anandibai), a high-caste widow who had attended the Sharada Sadan, and subsequently remarried another influential reformer in Bombay, Dhondo Keshav Karve. As well as establishing a number of girls' schools in Bombay, Karve opened a shelter for widows in 1896. This became a school that assisted widows to train for employment. See *Women in Modern India*, pp. 47 and 51.
she has studied and been trained as a teacher: Hindu reformers aimed to make widows independent and financially secure by providing them with skills that could be used in service to the community. See n. 56, *Widows' Home*.
'reformed' dress: Professional costume of the 'New Widow'—neat and businesslike, and in keeping with orthodoxy related to widows, unadorned.
he has returned home, via America, Japan and China: For early Hindu travellers, overseas travel was fraught with

anxieties about pollution and the possibility of losing caste. After the 1880s, it became increasingly common for western-educated Indians to study in London, and attitudes began to change. In her study of Indians travelling to England, Antoinette Burton writes: 'It could be argued that Indians exhibited aspirations to both Englishness and British citizenship by embarking on a kind of Grand Tour and producing narratives of that tour for consumption at home in India.' Most importantly, travel to and from Britain provided a conspicuous display of cosmopolitanism. Back home, these Indians published numerous guidebooks in India, commodifying Europe for a growing English-speaking market that was steadily acquiring the British habit of armchair tourism. See Burton, *At the Heart of the Empire*, pp. 11, 46, and 52.

57   *a quiet ceremony*: The formal marriage ceremony could also be very grandly organized.

58   *In this house you are installed as queen*: See also *Himself*, p. 209, where Justice Ranade teases his wife that she should exercise her liberty as 'Queen of the household' to eat without him.

59   *Book*: Ratanbai asserts herself as an equal partner in the marriage by claiming equal rights to the Book. See also Ranade, *Himself*, p. 83, where Taisasubai argues that: 'Nowadays, love means for a woman to boldly wrap her garment about her and be near her husband, to sit on a chair, to read and write like a man...'

his young partner's face: The western concept of companionate marriage was more readily acceptable to young Hindu men who had received a western-style education. Since intellectual companionship was dependent upon a similar style of education, wives and daughters were encouraged to imbue the model of 'the educated and cultured European wife'. See Heimsath, *Indian Nationalism*.

PANDITA RAMABAI
AND
THE PROBLEM OF INDIA'S
MARRIED WOMEN AND WIDOWS*

From time immemorial India has always abounded in prominent examples of good and great women. The praises of Sita, Draupadi, Savitri, Mirabai, Gayatri and hosts of others are sung in all languages; and even today, throughout the length and breadth of this our Bharatland, they are an inspiration to millions of women. In each period of the world's history these great leaders appear, who meet the peculiar needs of their own epoch. Pandita Ramabai stands out as one such leader in our own times. Her early training fitted her for the great service to which she was called. Her early education in her forest home where her mother was her teacher and her father her guide, her life of sorrow, her struggles, and finally her emergence on the platform of social reform, all these things show us clearly how God prepares His servants for His service.

In a newly discovered letter written in 1883 to Sir Bartle Frere, the Governor of Bombay, the Pandita gives a charmingly simple

---

* Taken from Shevantibai Nikambe, 'Pandita Ramabai and the Problem of India's Married Women and Widows' in *Women in Modern India*, collected and edited by Evelyn C. Gedge and Mithan Choksi (Bombay: D. B. Taraporewala Sons and Co., 1929), pp. 14–24.

account of her early life and childhood. She was born in a forest village of the western Ghats. Her father was a Shastri honoured for his learning in Mysore and in other states. In his youth he had studied under the teacher of the Peshwa Baji Rao II, and had so obtained entrance into the Peshwa's palace. There he had met the Peshwa's wife, Shreemati Varanesee Bai Sahiba, who was also learning Sanskrit with Rama Chandra Shastri. He had thus become interested in the question of women's education.

But though there was cultured ladies in the Mahratta place, when he came to the matter of teaching his wife and daughters, he found the village tradition strongly opposed to him. In the Pandita's words, 'The people in the neighbourhood disapproved of him, and threatened to put him out of caste. When they found they could in no way prevail with him to leave off educating my mother, they went to the Dharma-Guru (a spiritual ruler) and brought the matter before him, begging him to enforce the law against my father, because he was a breaker of their sacred laws and customs. So my father was sent for by the Dharma-Guru and was asked his reason for breaking the law. My father replied by asking the Dharma-Guru, "What is written in the Dharma Shastras which in any way forbids the education of women?" The Dharma-Guru could give no satisfactory answer, so my father remained in case.'

Several years after, when at Swade, the monastery of one of the Dharma-Gurus, many Pandits and one of the Dharma-Gurus were assembled to discuss the matter. There my father proved from the Dharma-Shastras that "women must be educated and learn their Dharma-Shastras." He received from the assembly a statement to this effect with their signatures affixed.

From her father Ramabai must have inherited, though in her case the goal was a very different one, her spirit of unswerving determination and devotion to an end. Anant Shastri had spent all his life in the service of religious contemplation and philosophical learning. Ten years he had spent seeking scholarship under the patronage of the Maharajahs of Mysore and Nepal; then years seeking religion and learning on pilgrimages; finally he had settled with his youthful second wife Lakshmibai in a lonely spot in the heart of the Gangamale forest where the sources of three rivers meet. The first nights they spent without the shelter of even a grass hut, with the jungle noises round them. Slowly they tamed the jungle and founded an *ashram*; roses, champak, mango, flourished in the heart of the jungle and persisted long after when the spot had been deserted, though now the jungle has once more resumed its sway, and not a trace remains of the *ashram* or the orchard or the cattle that Lakshmibai had administered so well.

Here, under her husband's tuition, Lakshmibai became so proficient in Sanskrit that she could in his absence carry on his work and instruct his *chelas*. It was in the forest hermitage that Ramabai was born, into an atmosphere, not only of unworldliness and idealism, but of courage and initiative. From her mother she must have inherited much of the organizing genius she was later to display in her great institute at Khedgaon.

About the time of her birth her father's mode of life was changed. In the forest *ashram*, as during his residence at the Maharajah's court, lavish gifts had been showered upon Anant Shastri; but money had meant nothing to him; it has been said of the family that none of them had any sense of their own interests, and finally the folly and greed of their relatives caused their financial ruin. The family sought means of livelihood and found it, as expounders of the Puranas or Sanskrit texts. They wandered on foot from place to place, traversing the whole of India, visiting places of pilgrimage, reading and expounding the sacred texts to groups of villagers, receiving for their livelihood the simple gifts that the poor brought to them. When she was a few months old, Ramabai started on her pilgrimage in a basket from the forest wilderness, and the wanderings continued till her parents' death. She received most of her education from her mother, and at the age of eight was already learning Sanskrit. Both she and her brother assisted in the reading of the *Puranas*. Her learning, and the fact that her father would not allow her to be married in her childhood, roused both wonder and hostility, even in their wanderings and more so when they occasionally settled in a village. The Pandita moved through all this, assimilating experience, watching with calm and critical eyes, unconsciously training herself for her life-work.

When her parents died in 1874, this village persecution caused the children to leave their home. There follows a graphic account of the wanderings of the brother and sister in the accomplishment of their missionary work. 'We travelled for six years in various parts of India. In our travels we were obliged to go on foot not having the means to afford conveyances. In this way we went a distance of two thousand miles. Thus we had a good opportunity of seeing the sufferings of Hindu women. We saw it not only in one part of India, but it was the same in the Madras Presidency, the Bombay Presidency, Punjab, the North-West Provinces, Bengal, Assam. This made us think much of how it was possible to improve the condition of women. We were able to do nothing directly to help them, but in the towns and cities we often addressed large audiences of people and urged upon them the education of the women and children. In order to be able to converse with the different races, we learnt Bengali and Hindi. In the year 1880 in Dacca my brother died, and then I was alone in the world.'

Six months later she married a Bengali gentleman who shared her enthusiasm for women's education. But after two years of happy comradeship and endeavour, he died, and she was left with a baby daughter and the debts incurred in building their new home where they had planned to live and work together.

But nothing could subdue her indomitable spirit. She planned to go to England to equip herself for her work of service to her country women. She sold the house, paid off her debts, and by publishing a book made enough money to pay for her passage.

But first she proceeded to Poona to be among people who spoke her own language. Here were working the most varying forces; a party of eager Hindu reformers were working ardently for the battle of women's freedom; on the other hand, the forces of reactionary orthodoxy were also very strong. Her fame as a Sanskrit scholar, her independence of action both before and after her marriage, had preceded her.

She was expected in the city with dread and dislike by the elderly women, with eager expectation by people like the Ranades, who saw in her a real women of the Upanishads, of the old day before degeneration. A slightly built woman with large steadfast eyes, her courage, her singlemindedness impressed itself upon all those who met her or who heard her speak. She had by now made up her mind to devote herself to the cause of her fellow-women. She made many friends among the leaders of the social reform movement, but she wished to proceed with greater audacity, greater impetus, than many of them. She decided to go to England and fit herself; by medical education, for the help of her fellow-women.

With the help of the Sisters of the Wantage Mission she came to England at last. A slight defect of hearing made it impossible for her to take the course in medicine that she had contemplated. At Cheltenham College she formed a lifelong friendship with that pioneer educationalist, Miss Beale; and here she perfected her knowledge of the English language and published a book, *The High Caste Hindu Woman*.

Ramabai went next to America, where her book had a wide circulation. American women, with their charm, eagerness and love for women of other lands, gave a great welcome to the Pandita, and took her to their hearts and homes. She stood before them, a fragile little woman clad in the spotless white flowing garb of ancient India, whither she proposed to return to work for the emancipation of widows.

Finally, equipped with funds and experience, Ramabai arrived in Bombay and opened an educational institution, the Sharada Sadan in a bungalow at Chowpatty, Bombay. There were present on this auspicious occasion many friends of female education, amongst whom were the most prominent of the Hindus. The entrance to the house was decorated with plantain trees, and yellow-flowered garlands told of emancipation for the oppressed widows for whom educational facilities were now provided.

It was the privilege of myself and my husband to be there that day and I will remember what a wonderful slight it seemed. The Pandita stood as hostess garbed in the white muslin of a Dakshini lady. Her hair was cut short, she wore no bangles on her arms, and her feet were clad in Brahman shoes without stockings. We were chiefly struck by the intellectuality of her brow, by her beautiful grey-blue eyes, and by her charming happy smile. She was true, she was noble, she was great. On this day, she was surrounded by grave Pandits, among whom were Rao Sahib Mandlik, Rao Sahib V. A. Modak, The Hon. Mr Justice K. T. Telang, Dr Bhandarkar, Mr Chandavarkar, and others, all of whom were keenly interested in the cause of women's education.

The Sharada Sadan was so called from one of the names of the Goddess Saraswati, the goddess of Learning and Wisdom; to this House of Wisdom came numerous high-caste girls and persecuted young widows. After having become a Theist, the Pandita had adopted Christianity and the Sadan became a Christian Institution.

Great as its work was, it still seemed circumscribed to the Pandita's great spirit. With the terrible famine of 1896 came a vast extension. She had herself suffered terrific privations from famine during her wander years. She had begged food for her dying mother, and had lived with her brother on roots and wild berries. She departed now for the stricken area. The first sight of three little famished skeleton-like forms determined her in her resolve to admit into her institution all the destitute girls who needed refuge. 'The Lord has put it into my heart to save three hundred girls out of the famine districts and I shall go to work in His name. The funds sent to me by my friends in America are barely enough to feed and educate fifty girls and several people are asking me how I am going to support all these girls who may come from Central India. But the Lord knows what I need.' Her helpers at the Sadan received loyally the burden of their new charges, wild, undisciplined, illiterate girls. When the Pandita returned, she organized at Khedgaon, near Poona, the Mukti Sadan, or House of Salvation. It meant an almost complete retirement along with these girls, from the active intellectual stimulus of life at Poona. But as the Pandita said, 'There is no room for murmuring.'

In time, all the work was concentrated at Khedgaon. The Sharada Sadan was transferred there as part of the larger project. It continued its work of providing higher education for girls who could take advantage of it. But the reach of the Pandita's compassion was henceforth unlimited. A third department was opened, the Kripa Sadan or Rescue Home.

In 1900, with the Gujerat famine, came a new time of trial and test. Twenty of her helpers went out to the area, 'Eight of them women who had been saved from starvation in 1896.' When she had had resources in 1896 for fifty girls, she had admitted three hundred. Now she had resources for five or six hundred, and she admitted thirteen hundred and fifty, bringing the total population at Mukti up to nineteen hundred, 'with over a hundred cattle.' With the help of a hundred and fifty devoted young women, she dealt with this new situation. A school was organized with over fifty classes and teachers. Four hundred children were occupied in the Kindergarten. A Training School for Teachers was opened, and an Industrial School with garden, fields, oil-press, dairy, laundry, departments for baking, sewing, weaving, and embroidery. For those who could only do very coarse work there were grain-parching, tinning culinary utensils, dyeing.

It was a wonderful piece of organization. We are told that the Pandita's day began well before four o'clock in the morning, during the last twenty-two years. One can well believe it. Never were the gates of the Sadan shut to any who were in need. And yet in this vast work of organizing, she never lost her serenity and her spirituality; no sign of bustle or worry marred the repose of her beautiful spirit. Her nights were spent in prayer and vigil; her great aim was to bring joyousness and blessedness into the lives of these girls, often so untrained, sullen, gross on their first admission. She never forgot this in the detail of management of this large-scale work. Through the busy, bustling life of the place moved the slight serene figure with the great brow and the wide grey eyes, her spirit soaring above age, sorrow, labour, till at last she was called in 1922 to the rest she had always denied herself.

My own work for married ladies began when I joined Pandita Ramabai's staff in Bombay. When she moved her school to Poona, I remained in Bombay and gradually developed the Married Women's School which has now been in existence for sixteen years, during which time 1000 women have taken advantage of the school courses; amongst whom have been child wives and widows in large numbers, also the wives of many professional men.

The married woman in India presents a problem. As a rule she is not given much chance for education as she is bound by caste and tradition and she is called upon to fulfil solemn duties and responsibilities long before she is fit for them. Homes being sacred temples, the Hindu woman is in the right sense of the term a priestess in her own house.

Home is also the first school of every child, the mother being the child's first teacher. It is therefore very important to bring enlightenment and a fitting training to the married women, so that the foundations of home life may be truly built. Every girl's natural ambition is to possess her own home, but if she should become a widow her life can be consecrated to some special service for her country, such as has been rendered in the West by sisterhoods or cloisters. Widows have been sent for specialized training in colleges or hospitals where they learn to be teachers or nurses.

The work of my school has met with support from both government and the general public. The success of this work in Bombay proves, I think, that special schools for married women might well be attached to every primary or high school for girls in which general and special courses of study are being followed.

Educated women are waking up to their real responsibilities in public matters and, provided there is right guidance and proper organization, there is hope that some of the trying problems which affect women may be solved through an improvement in public opinion which has been brought about by extended education. Women who have become alive to the needs of their sisters are seeking opportunities for helpfulness and efforts are being made to break the bonds of custom and caste. In such work lies a most important sphere for the married woman and the widow. If educated on proper lines these women will prove to be the fit ones to solve all the great and small problems that involve the progress and prosperity of our land.

This call then is to the married women and widows. Let them in their leisure hours take up their duties, let them form committees and organize and open classes and special schools for widows and married women and as far as is possible let the teachers in such schools be married women. Education has so far advanced that it is possible for the married woman to spare her leisure hours for this important work.

There is no need to wait for government or municipalities to take the lead. It is the duty of individual women to start such work and government and municipalities should supplement the funds.

Public bodies however do not need educated women on their committees as much as those are needed on the committees of homes and families. It is in the home that the prime duty of the mother and wife lies.

Let us then seek out those and give them educational relief and then mark the changes which will follow.

Two royal ladies, one a Maharani and the other a Navab Shah Begum have come forward to take the lead and it is hoped that many others will follow them.

No structure dare be built without a solid foundation and that foundation is brave wives and mothers; therefore let us offer as many facilities as possible for the married women and widows that they may advance along the right lines and fulfil the needs of that noble domain the HOME with its many responsibilities.

BIBLIOGRAPHY

PUBLICATIONS BY SHEVANTIBAI NIKAMBE

Ratanbai: A Sketch of a Bombay High Caste Hindu Young Wife (London: Marshall Brothers, 1895).

'Pandita Ramabai and The Problem of India's Married Women and Widows' in *Women in Modern India*, collected and edited by Evelyn C. Gedge and Mithan Choksi (Bombay: D. B. Taraporewala Sons and Co, 1929), pp. 14–24 (Reproduced in this edition).

REVIEWS ON THE FIRST EDITION OF *RATANBAI*

'Child-Wives in India' in *The Daily News*, London, 20 July 1895, p. 6.

'The Hindu Girl-Wife' in *The Daily Chronicle*, London, 24 July 1895.

'Book World' in *The Christian*, London, 18 July, p. 22.

OTHER REFERENCES

Chandani Lokugé, *Between the Idea and the Reality: A Study of Late Nineteenth and Early Twentieth Century Indian-English Women's Fiction*, PhD thesis, Flinders University of South Australia, 1993, pp. 124–50.

——— 'The Genesis of the Indian Women's English Literary Tradition: Fostering Interest and Research', in Cynthia vanden Driesan and Satendra Nandan, *Austral-Asian Encounters: From Literature and Women's Studies to Politics and Tourism* (New Delhi: Prestige, 2003), pp. 296–304.

Dorothy M. Spencer, *Indian Fiction in English, An Annotated Bibliography* (Philadelphia: University of Pennsylvania Press, 1960), p. 32.

K. S. Ramamurti, *Rise of the Indian Novel in English* (New Delhi: Sterling, 1987), pp. 79–80.

Eunice de Souza (ed.), 'Introduction', in *Ratanbai: A Sketch of a Bombay High Caste Hindu Young Wife* by Shevantibai Nikambe (New Delhi: Sahitya Akademi, 2003), pp. 1–12.

Eunice de Souza and Lindsay Pereira (eds), *Women's Voices: Selections from Nineteenth and Early-Twentieth Century Indian Writing in English* (New Delhi: Oxford University Press, 2002), pp. 58–65.